力得文化
Leader Culture

International Trade English
FOR SALES

國貿B.C.S.英語

A咖國貿人

施美怡◎著

深植就業力+升值職場競爭力

A咖國貿人的必備指南

由業務往來 **Business Contacts**、商務活動 **Commercial Activities** 和社交公關 **Social Intercourse**引領你進入國貿業務世界，在人際互動上更無往不利。

- 【情境對話】: 提升你英文口語能力 ⇒ **商務社交不打結**
- 【關鍵字彙、句型】: 擴充國貿專業語彙和英語詞彙 ⇒ **書到用時不恨少**
- 【勵志小格言】: 名人佳句、砥志礪行 ⇒ **邁向目標無往不利**
- 【職場經驗談+菜鳥變達人】: **全面提升國貿專業能力** ⇒ **成為【A咖國貿人】指日可待**

作者序

您是否也像作者一樣，年輕時總在新年的開始對自己許下願望，期許自己精進英文，但卻也總是給自己許多的藉口，最後虎頭蛇尾，無疾而終呢？蘋果公司創辦人賈伯斯（Steve Jobs）說：「你想花你的餘生賣糖水，還是想要個可以改變世界的機會？（Do you want to spend the rest of your life selling sugared water or do you want a chance to change the world？）」。也許你我沒有改變世界這樣遠大的志向，但可以改變自己。

前一冊的《國貿英文說寫一本通》主要是以國貿流程為架構，以「買方（進口商）」及「賣方（出口商）」的角度帶入主題式【情境對話】及【英文書信】，本書以同樣的架構為基礎，談論除了國貿流程外，其它貿易實務中會碰觸到的商務主題，同樣在【知識補給】及【職場經驗談】單元提供商用知識及分享實務經驗，並且加入新的單元【勵志小格言】，不論是在生活、學習及就業等等各方面鼓勵讀者。

給自己一個改變的機會，而且就從此時此刻立即啟動學習/改變計畫吧！

施美怡

編者序

《國貿英語說寫一本通 - 業務篇》包含了國貿業務所需知道的知識，由業務往來、商務活動和社交公關三大章節所組成，更符合國貿業務所需要的綜合素養。另一方面，除了要有國貿理論與實務的知識經驗之外，語言能力更是這個產業的核心競爭力，本書中包含了對話和書信為主的架構，切中了在商用書信上和國外客戶直接溝通所需要的能力，更有助於英語能力的提升。

《國貿英語說寫一本通 - 業務篇》在架構上藉由【情境說明】、【情境對話】、【中文翻譯】、【關鍵字彙】、【關鍵句型】、【勵志小格言】以及【英文書信這樣寫】、【知識補給】、【職場經驗談】、【菜鳥變達人】等單元，讓您晉升為 A 咖國貿業務，全面提升國貿專業能力以及英語力。

力得文化編輯群

CONTENTS 目次

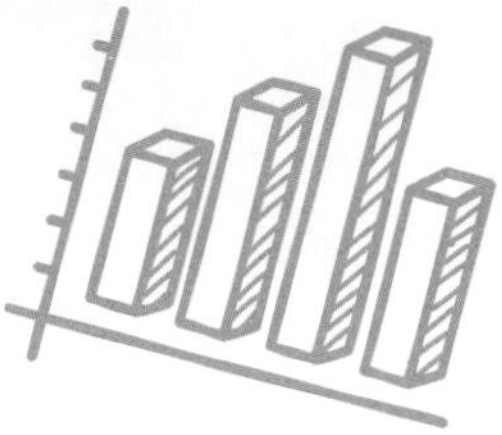

Part 1 業務往來 Business Contacts

1-1 維繫舊客戶 Existing Customer Maintenance

1-2 開發新客戶 New Customer Development

1-3 新產品開發
New Product Development

Part2 商務活動 Commercial Activities

2-1 參加商展
Participation in the Trade Exhibition

目次 CONTENTS

2-2 商務旅行 Business Travel

2-3 客戶來訪 Visitation

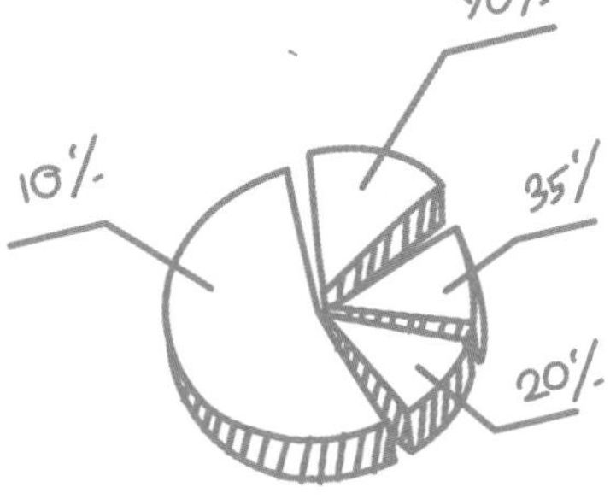

Part3 社交公關 Social Intercourse

3-1 公告通知 Announcement and Notification

3-2 人際互動 Interpersonal Communication

1-1 維繫舊客戶
Existing Customer Maintenance

1-2 開發新客戶
New Customer Development

1-3 新產品開發
New Product Development

業務往來
Business Contacts

Part 1

1-1 維繫舊客戶
Existing Customer Maintenance

1-1-1 產品介紹（對既有客戶）
Product Introduction to Existing Customer

★情境說明

Best Corp. introduces product to ABC Co.

倍斯特公司向ABC公司介紹產品

★角色介紹

（買方）Buyer: ABC Co., Ltd.

（賣方）Seller: Best International Trade Corp.

情境對話

B: This is balancing valve we've been discussing during the exhibition.	B: 這是上次展覽中我們所討論的平衡閥。
A: It looks heavy, but actually it isn't. What's the material and process used to fabricate this design?	A: 看起來很重，實際卻不然。此產品是採用什麼材質及製程？

B: We use the new material composed by local brass supplier. It's a more stable material for brass forging process.

B: 所使用的是本地供應商調配的新材質。此材質更趨穩定，適合鍛造製程。

A: How's your product better than other competitors'?

A: 你們的產品於哪方面優於其他競爭者？

B: As what I've said just now, the part has been forged. Forging provides an economical alternative to casting by other suppliers.

B: 如我方才所提及，此產品是用鍛造製程，比起其他供應商的鑄造製程，鍛造製程是一個經濟實惠的選擇。

A: Sounds impressive. How about its quality?

A: 聽起來很吸引人。產品質量如何？

B: The design has passed the test of its basic function. Testing includes many aspects, such as function testing and performance testing. We achieve both price concession and quality assurance.

B: 此設計已經通過基本功能測試，測試項目涵蓋許多層面，包含功能測試及性能測試。我們同時達到價格優惠與品質保證。

A: If your price can be more favorable, we can place a trial order right away.

A: 如果貴司的價格能更優惠，我們可以馬上下一張試用訂單。

關鍵字彙

process *(n.)* [`prɑsɛs] 過程

同義詞 operation, course, step

相關詞 in the process of 在…過程中；development process 開發過程

fabricate *(v.)* [`fæbrɪˏket] 製造

同義詞 manufacture, construct, build

相關詞 fabricated construction 裝配式施工；fabricating cost 造價

compose *(v.)* [kəm`poz] 組成

同義詞 make up, form, constitute

相關詞 composed of 由…組成，compose oneself 鎮靜

economical *(a.)* [ˏikə`nɑmɪk!] 經濟的

同義詞 money-saving, cost-effective, low-cost

相關詞 economical load 經濟負載；economical constraint 經濟限制

impressive *(a.)* [ɪm`prɛsɪv] 令人印象深刻的

同義詞 amazing, awesome, awe-inspiring

相關詞 impressive force 威風，impressive achievement 了不起的成就

aspect *(n.)* [`æspɛkt] 方面、觀點

同義詞 field, respect, side

相關詞 multi – aspect 多方位；main aspects 要領

關鍵句型

As what sb.'ve said 如某人所述

例句說明

As what you've said, quality assurance is the key point.

➡ 如同你所述，品質保證是重點。

As what I've said, customer's satisfaction is our greatest achievement.

➡ 如我所述，客戶滿意是我們最大滿足。

替換句型

Like I said, customer's satisfaction is our greatest achievement.

both A and B 兩者都

例句說明

The law protects **both** the buyer **and** the seller.

➡ 法律保護買賣雙方。

On-line shopping is **both** cheap **and** convenient.

➡ 線上購物既便宜又方便。

替換句型

The law protects not only the buyer but also the seller.

勵志小格言

Experience is not what happens to a man; it is what a man does with what happens to him.

~By Aldous Leonard Huxley, American writer

經驗不會從天而降；經驗只有通過實踐才能獲得。 *~美國作家　赫克利斯*

英文書信這樣寫

Dear Olivia,

It was nice to receive your phone call this morning and learn that you are interested in our connector, one of our best selling items in the market.

What makes this type a hot sale item is its convenient operation by one-hand assembly for quick installation. The model also achieve greater security by success in pressure testing with much higher standard than common industry security requirements. It's more reliable and efficacious function and greatly reduces any possible leakage problems, and provide security and protection.

Attached are the detailed specification and price list for two versions of high-functional connector : CH0001 for balance valve and CH0002 for ball valve. As you can tell, both offer flexibility with their fitting products and both are competitively priced. In view of fact that we have cooperated with each other for many years, we'll give you an extra special discount of 5 percent for this item.

We appreciate your support in these years and look forward to your response.

Yours sincerely,
Wesley Yang

中文翻譯

奧莉維亞您好，

很高興今早接到您的來電，並獲知貴司對我司的連接器感興趣，這款產品是我們在市場中最熱銷的品項之一。

操作方便，可單手組裝，以達到快速安裝的目的，致使這款產品炙手可熱。此設計也通過壓力測試，測試標準高於一般工業安全要求。其更可靠及有效的功能大大降低了任何可能的洩漏問題，並提供安全和保護。

附件為兩個版本的高功能連接器的詳細的規格和價目表：CH0001適用於平衡閥及CH0002 適用於球閥。如您所視，兩個版本皆可與其配合產品靈活組配，且價格具競爭力。鑒於我們雙方合作多年，我司將針對此款產品，提供貴司額外百分之五的優惠折扣。

感謝貴司這些年來的支持。靜候佳音！

衛斯理　楊　敬啟

知識補給

從事國際貿易業務，撥打國際電話給客戶或出差時撥打電話回台灣，為家常便飯，除了要了解撥打國際電話的方法外，撥打電話時亦須特別留意時差問題，避免造成受話方的困擾。可參考下列國內電信業者網站提供查詢各國國碼、區碼、時差，及通話費率 http://www.cht.com.tw/portal/rateFinder

從國內撥打國際電話至國外：國際冠碼（例如：002，依各電信公司有所區別）+ 國碼 + 區域號碼（區域號碼前之0不須撥）+ 電話號碼

例如：由台灣直撥美國紐約 – 002 + 1 + 212 + 123 4567

從國外撥打國際電話回國內：當地國際冠碼 + 國碼 + 區域號碼（區域號碼前之0不須撥）+ 電話號碼

例如：由紐約直撥台北 – 011 + 886 + 2 + 2222 3333

職場經驗談

向客戶介紹產品主要要點在強調產品特色，如性能、質量、功能及價格等，說明與其他競爭者產品的差異化，藉此吸引買家的興趣，尤其對於往來交易多年的合作夥伴，可提供特別優惠方案，藉此感謝對方的支持及鞏固雙方合作關係，最後務必表達積極等待對方回應及建立商業關係。

菜鳥變達人

中翻英練習

1. 如您所述，低價格及高品質永遠是重點。

2. 我們同時關心價格與質量。

中翻英解答

1. As what you've said, low price and high quality are always important.
2. Both prices and quality are we concerned about.

1-1-2 新品上市
Notification of New Product Launch

★情境說明

Best Corp. notifies ABC Co. of the new product launch.
倍斯特公司通知ABC公司其新品上市。

★角色介紹

（買方）Buyer: ABC Co., Ltd.
（賣方）Seller: Best International Trade Corp.

情境對話

B: I'm pleased to tell you that we have been successful in manufacturing a new type valve.

B: 非常高興的通知您，我公司已成功製造完成新型閥門。

A: What's the difference between new type and original one?

A: 新款與舊款的區別為何？

B: The new type regulates the flow of water more efficiently and can apply to high temperature and pressure valves media.

B: 新型閥門更有效地控制水流量，並且適用於高溫高壓介質。

A: Sounds great. But we are much more concerned about if it can be functioned steadily.

A: 聽起來好極了。但我們更關心的是功能穩定。

B: The functional test and performance test were carried out to ensure the function meets requirements. We think there will be a substantial market opportunity for the new product with excellent performance.

B: 我們已完成了功能測試以及性能測試，確保功能符合需求。我們相信這款超高性能的新品將有極大的市場機會。

A: What are other selling points?

A: 還有什麼其它賣點？

B: At the sales promotion stage of new product, we're going to allow you 3% discount.

B: 在新品促銷階段，我們將提供貴司3%折扣。

A: Now it is more than inspiring.

A: 現在更吸引人了。

關鍵字彙

apply to *(ph.)* **適用於**

同義詞 be useful for, be applicable to

相關詞 apply to recruit 適用於新職工；apply to all parts 適用於所有產品

carry out *(ph.)* **完成**

同義詞 accomplish, execute, fulfill

相關詞 carry out the work 完成工作；carry out maintenance 完成維護

substantial *(a.)* [səb`stænʃəl] **極大的**

同義詞 fairly large, significant, substantive

相關詞 substantial change 重大變革；substantial loss 重大損失

market opportunity *(ph.)* **市場機會**

相關詞 market demand 市場需求；market development 市場開發

解析 市場機會 (market opportunity) 是指市場上存在尚未滿足或尚未完全滿足的需求，換言之就是市場上對某產品仍有全部或部份需求。

excellent *(n.)* [`ɛks!ənt] **優秀的**

同義詞 extraordinary, outstanding, superior

相關詞 excellent quality 優質；excellent terms of employment 優異的薪酬條款

selling points *(ph.)* **賣點**

同義詞 point

相關詞 major selling point 最大賣點；best selling point 最佳賣點

promotion stage *(ph.)* **促銷階段**

相關詞 initial stage of the promotion 促銷初期

解析 促銷（Sales Promotion）是指對同業或消費者提供短程激勵，以誘使購買某種特定商品的活動，一般簡稱為SP。

關鍵句型

be successful in sth. 在某方面獲得成功

例句說明

Jack **is** highly **successful in** business.

➡ 傑克經商相當成功。

Our company **was successful in** negotiating lower prices.

➡ 我司就降價，談判成功。

替換句型

Our company achieved success in negotiating lower prices.

Sb. be much more concerned about sth. 某人更在意某事

例句說明

Customers **are much more concerned about** product quality.

➡ 客戶更在意產品質量。

My supervisor **is much more concerned about** my performance.

➡ 主管更在意我的表現。

替換句型

My supervisor is much more conscious about my performance.

勵志小格言

Living without an aim is like sailing without a compass.

~ By Alexander Dumas, Davy de La Pailleterie, French Writer

生活沒有目標就像航海沒有指南針。

～法國作家　大仲馬

英文書信這樣寫

Dear Sir and Madam,

We're very pleased to inform you about our new balancing valve designed by our R&D team.

The new type has improved the function to be more stable and efficient. In view of high-quality and low-price, we think that the new type will be very competitive and well-received in the market.

Please never hesitate to contact us if you'd like to know more about production information.

Yours sincerely,
Wesley Yang

中文翻譯

敬啟者：

我們公司非常高興通知您，我們研發部門開發出了新型平衡閥。

新型產品改良了產品功能，使其更穩定及更有效率。基於物美價廉，相信它將很有競爭力，且在市場上受到青睞。

如欲瞭解更多產品資訊，請儘管與我司聯絡。

衛斯理　楊　敬啟

知識補給

電子郵件發送時會自動產生寄件人姓名及電郵地址（等同郵寄信件的信頭／Heading）及日期（Date），因此電子郵件中只需包含 1. 收件人稱呼（Salutation）、2. 開頭語（Opening）、3. 本文（Body）、4. 結束語（Concluding）、5. 敬語（Complimentary Close）以及6. 簽名（Signature），範例說明如下。

收件者：abc@abc.com
副本：olivia-palermo@abc.com
主旨：New Product Launch
附件：

Dear Sir and Madam, *1.收件人稱呼（Salutation）*

We're very pleased to inform you about our new balancing valve designed by our R&D team. *2. 開頭語（Opening）*

The function of the new type has improved more stable and efficient. In view of high-quality and low-price, we think that the new type will be very competitive and well received in the market. *3. 本文（Body）*

Please never hesitate to contact us if you'd like to know more about production information. *4. 結束語（Concluding）*

Yours Sincerely, *5. 敬語（Complimentary Close）*
Wesley Yang *6. 簽名（Signature）*
Product Manager
Best International Trade Corp.

職場經驗談

隨著時代變遷、科技進步及網際網路的普及，現行商業活動已鮮少使用郵寄信件作為溝通往來方式，大多藉由電子郵件作為溝通工具，甚至隨著智慧型手機的廣泛運用，有些更利用 Line、WhatsApp、WeChat 等軟體達到即時溝通的目的。無論使用何種溝通工具，務必切記「口說無憑」，在雙方進行討論後，建議補上一封電子郵件詳載雙方討論過之內容，作為依據。

菜鳥變達人

中翻英練習

1. 她在貿易領域上相當成功。

2. 經理更在意你的表現。

中翻英解答

1. She is highly successful in the trade area.
2. The manager is much more concerned about your performance.

1-1-3 產品停產
Notification of Production Suspense

★情境說明

Best Corp. notifies ABC Co. of suspending production.
倍斯特公司通知ABC公司其產品停產。

★角色介紹

（買方）Buyer: ABC Co., Ltd.
（賣方）Seller: Best International Trade Corp.

情境對話

B: I'm calling to inform you that our P/N 0003 will ease production.

B: 我打電話來是為了通知您，我司編號003的產品將減產。

A: It would be difficult for us to accept this news. We still have future forecast on this product, as this type has dominated the market for many years.

A: 收到此訊息令我們難以接受。我們對此產品仍有預估需求，這個款式已主導市場多年。

B: Suspending production is mainly due to the problem of sourcing the raw materials.

B: 停產主要來自原料取得問題。

A: What are the alternatives?

A: 有什麼替代品？

B: There are several types with similar functionality. I will send you the related product information later.

B: 有幾款具類似功能的產品。稍後我會將產品相關資料寄給您。

A: When is the latest order date?

A: 最後下單日為何？

B: April 20th is the deadline for placing order. We're trying to keep low stock level during the production. From then on, we will make an inventory of the warehouse.

B: 4月20日為下單截止日。我們試著在生產過程中降低庫存水準，之後再清點庫存。

A: I am delighted to absorb your inventory. Let us know the final quantity, once firmed.

A: 我非常樂意吸收貴公司的庫存，讓我知道確認的最終數量。

關鍵字彙

ease *(v.)* [iz] 緩和

同義詞 allay, alleviate , reduce

相關詞 ease economic crisis 緩和經濟危機；ease restrictions 寬鬆出口限制

dominate *(v.)* [\`dɑmə͵net] 主導

同義詞 allocate, control, monopolize

相關詞 dominate investment flows 主導投資流動；dominate the world economy 主導世界經濟

firm *(v.)* [fɝm] 堅固

同義詞 solidify, stabilize

相關詞 firm offer 確定價；firm up the agreement 把協議確定下來

suspend production *(ph.)* 停產

同義詞 go out of production, run down , stop production

相關詞 in mass production 量產；under production 減產

alternative *(n.)* [ɔl\`tɝnətɪv] 選擇、二擇一

同義詞 choice, replacement, substitute

相關詞 have no alternative but 除…外別無選擇；alternative source 替代原料

stock level *(ph.)* 庫存水準

同義詞 inventory level

相關詞 safety stock 安全庫存

解析 庫存控制的作用主要是在保證企業生產、經營需求的前提下，使庫存量經常保持在合理的水準上，以掌握庫存量動態，避免超儲或缺貨。

absorb *(v.)* [əbˋsɔrb] **吸收**

同義詞 resorb, imbibe, take in

相關詞 absorb money 收起現金；absorb production in excess 吸收多餘生產

關鍵句型

be difficult for us to accept⋯. 難以接受 ⋯.

Your offer is too high, which **is difficult for us to accept**.

➡ 貴司的報價太高了，我方難以接受。

I'm afraid **it will be difficult for us to** reduce the prices.

➡ 我恐怕降價會有所困難。

替換句型

I can't adapt well to your high offer.

Sb. be delighted to⋯ 樂於⋯

例句說明

I'd be absolutely delighted to visit your company.

➡ 我非常樂意去拜訪貴司。

Kate was delighted to meet you.

➡ 凱特非常高興見到您。

替換句型

Kate was glad to meet you.

勵志小格言

Everything comes if a man will only wait.

天下無難事，只怕有心人。

解析：沒有克服不了的困難，只要有決心，凡事都能解決。

英文書信這樣寫

Dear Customers,

This notification is about the end of production.

Due to the shortage of raw materials, we have decided to discontinue three models of ball valve, said P/N 0011, 0012, and 0013. Taking into account the demands of the market, we expect to launch out new product in this series in the second quarter. We'll keep you advised of the related information, once available.

Best Industrial is deeply grateful for your support of these products.

Yours Sincerely,
Wesley Yang

中文翻譯

親愛的客戶：

特此奉告產品停產。

由於原物料短缺，我司決定停產三款球閥產品，分別是產品編號 0011，0012，以及0013。考量到市場需求，我司預計在第二季上市同系列新品。待新品完成，我司將會通知您相關訊息。

倍斯特工業深摯地感激您對該產品的支持。

衛斯理　楊　敬啟

知識補給

在前一章節中說明了書信的基本架構，在這裡我們將詳細說明商業書信中常用的稱謂，即「收件人稱呼（Salutation）」。

- ✔ 統稱：適用於統一信函寄發給多位客戶，如尾牙邀請函、休假公告等。例如：Dear Sir（親愛的先生）、Dear Madam（親愛的女士）、Dear Sir and Madam（敬啟者）、Dear Customers（親愛的客戶）。
- ✔ 姓氏 + 先生／女士之稱謂：適用於較不熟悉或首次聯繫之客戶。例如Dear Mr. Lee（親愛的李先生）、Dear Miss／Ms. Lee（親愛的李小姐／女士）、Dear Mrs. Lee（親愛的李夫人）、Dear Mr. and Mrs.（親愛的李氏賢伉儷）。
- ✔ 姓名 + 先生／女士之稱謂：適用於較熟悉之客戶。例如Dear Mr. John Lee（親愛的李約翰先生）、Dear Miss／Ms. Annie Lee（親愛的李安妮小姐）。
- ✔ 名字不加任何稱謂：適用於長期合作、關係密切之客戶。例如Dear John（親愛的約翰）、Dear Annie（親愛的安妮）。

職場經驗談

「產品停產通知」為商業書信中重要的書信之一，產品停產將可能引起客戶端供貨短缺，也關係著供應商與客戶間是否會持續合作的關係。因此產品停產通知除了要詳載停產的產品品號、顏色、規格及停產日期，並告知停產的原因及最後下單日期，讓客戶能及早鋪貨及備庫。另外，最好能提供「補救方案」，例如推薦類似規格的既有產品或預告即將開發的等同規格新品等，以維持與客戶後續之合作關係。

菜鳥變達人

中翻英練習

1. 我們覺得很難接受出貨一再延遲。

2. 我司很樂意協助貴司度過財務困境。

中翻英解答

1. We find it difficult to accept the shipment had been delayed again.
2. We would be delighted to help you over all the finance difficulties.

1-1-4 恢復往來
Business Resuming

★情境說明

Best Corp. contacts Jackson Industrial Inc. whom stopped ordering of long standing, to resume business.

倍斯特公司聯繫久未下單的傑克森工業，以恢復業務往來。

★角色介紹

（買方）Buyer: Jackson Industrial

（賣方）Seller: Best International Trade Corp.

情境對話

J: You've reached Jackson Industrial. This is Amanda Howard.

J: 這裡是傑克森工業，我是艾曼達 霍華德。

B: Hello, Amanda. This is Wesley Yang from Best Corp. It's quite a long time I haven't kept in touch with you, and what have you been up to?

B: 你好，艾曼達。我是倍斯特公司的衛斯理 楊，有好長一段時間沒有妳的消息，近來如何？

J: Bonjour, Wesley. I'm dedicated to making a promotional advertising campaign for Christmas. Is there anything I can help?

J: 你好，衛斯理。我正忙於為耶誕節做廣告促銷計畫。有什麼我可以幫忙的嗎？

B: I'd like to know if there's any difficulty on the sale of our product that stop you ordering. It's against our business philosophy to see our old customers like you not placing as regular orders as you are in the past.

B: 我想知道貴司在銷售我們的產品上是否有任何困難，致使貴司停止訂購。看到像貴司這樣的老客戶不再像過去那樣定期下單，這有違我們的經營理念。

J: Generally speaking, the quality of your product and service is quite good. However, your price is much higher than other competitors

J: 大致而言，貴司的產品和服務品質是很好的。然而，貴司的價格比其他競爭對手高。

B: Although our prices seem higher, our high-quality products are worth having in consideration of long-term benefit. Incidentally, here's a good piece of news. Our development in new product got a runaway success; we are going to give priority to offering special discounts of our old business partner.

B: 儘管我們的價格似乎偏高，就長期利益來說，高品質的產品是值得擁有的。順道一提一個好消息。我們的新產品開發一舉成功，我們將優先提供我們的老商業夥伴新產品的特別折扣。

J: Well. That sounds a bit attractive. Please send me the updated catalogue and price list.

J: 嗯，這聽起來有點吸引力。請給我貴司最新的目錄和價格表。

關鍵字彙

dedicated to *(ph.)* 致力於；專心於

同義詞 devoted to；loyal to；loving towards

相關詞 dedicate oneself to 獻身於；dedicated to work 投入工作

promotional *(a.)* [prə`moʃən!] 促銷的；宣傳

同義詞 of publicizing

相關詞 promotional video 宣傳影片；promotional material 促銷品

advertise *(v.)* [`ædvɚ͵taɪz] 為…廣告；為…宣傳

同義詞 publicise, promote

相關詞 advertise job offers 招聘；advertising cost 廣告費

against *(prep.)* [ə`gɛnst] 反對；違反

同義詞 versus; opposite; leaning on

相關詞 against inflation 抑止通貨膨脹；stand against 反對

philosophy *(n.)* [fə`lɑsəfɪ] 原理；人生觀

同義詞 belief

相關詞 philosophy of hard work 刻苦的作風

runaway success *(ph.)* 大獲全勝；一舉成功

同義詞 devastating success; overwhelming victory

相關詞 runaway best – seller 搶手暢銷書；runaway prices 飛漲的價格

關鍵句型

what have you been up to 在忙些什麼？(表達問候對方近來如何)

例句說明

What have you been up to recently?

➡ 最近在忙些什麼？

替換句型

What have you been doing recently?

What has kept you busy recently?

What are you occupied recently?

give priority to 優先考慮

例句說明

Our next goal should give priority to the development of new product.

➡ 我們下一步要優先發展新品。

To avoid quality defect, we should give priority to root cause.

➡ 避免品劣品需先找出根源。

替換句型

The development of new product is the top priority as our next goal.

勵志小格言

In this world there is always danger for those who are afraid of it.

～ *George Bernard Shaw, Playwright*

在這個世界上，害怕的人永遠都會遇上危險。 ～ *劇作家　蕭伯納*

英文書信這樣寫

Dear Amanda,

How is everything? I re-ran in my mind our accounts for the past year, and note that we have not received neither information nor orders from you for a long time.

Assuming that your company is still operating in the series of our production, please inform us of your recent sales intention and goal for our reference. In case you have any comments or suggestions about our products to order, please do not hesitate to put forward to our company, for the benefit of our company as review and improvement.

We presume that your company must be willing to learn that our products make a series of upgrade, but in technology and functions. Enclosed are the updated catalogue and price list, including the new models of the line you used to order. You'll find out our products are in line with your needs just well and be quite satisfied with them. Furthermore, the same series of samples have been in transit for your inspection.

We look forward to receiving your positive response and resuming our friendly business connections.

Yours sincerely,
Wesley Yang

中文翻譯

艾曼達您好，

一切都好嗎？我在腦海中回顧雙方過往的紀錄，發現我司已有很長一段時間沒有收到貴司的訊息及訂單了。

假設貴司仍在經營我司生產的系列產品，請告知貴司近期的銷售目的和目標，供我司參考。若貴司對向我司訂購產品有任何意見及建議，請不吝向我們公司提出，以利我司作為檢討及改善的參考

相信貴司一定樂於獲知我司的產品在技術上及功能上做出了一系列的提升。附件是更新的產品目錄及價格表，其中包含貴司以往訂購的系列產品的新款式。貴司將會發現我司產品正符合貴司需要，並會對它們相當滿意。此外同一系列樣品已寄出予貴司檢視。

我司期待收到貴司回覆，以及雙方恢復友好業務關係。

衛斯理　楊　敬啟

知識補給

商業書信基本架構中主要內文包含三個部分：

✔ 開頭語（Opening）：表達問候及發文依據或源由。常用開頭語：

- This is to acknowledge of your email dated Jan. 1, 2015.
- We are glad / regret to learn from your email of Jan. 1, 2015.
- We regret to remind you that…
- By this opportunity we'd like to inform you that…
- With reference to your email dated Jan. 1, 2015,…
- This is a follow-up to our email dated Jan. 1, 2015, in which…

✔ 本文（Body）：闡明信文主題。

✔ 結束語（Concluding）：對該文的後續處理行動。常用結束語：

- We look forward to hearing from you soon.
- Your attention to this email will be greatly appreciated.
- Please accept our apology for any inconvenience we have caused you.
- We assure you of our prompt attention to your needs.
- Shall there be any inquiry, please never hesitate to email us.
- Your prompt reply to this inquiry will be appreciated.

職場經驗談

對於許久無業務往來之客戶以問候對方為優先，才不至於令對方覺得唐突，而後表達關切中斷往來之原因，例如是否我方服務不周或者對方業務項目變更等。最後進而表達期盼持續合作關係之渴望。

菜鳥變達人

中翻英練習

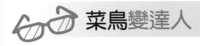

1. 你們必須優先解決這一個問題。

2. 我司優先錄用有經驗的應徵者。

中翻英解答

1.You should give priority to such a problem.

2.Our company give priority to experienced applicants.

1-1-5 同意代理
Agreement for Exclusive Agency

★情境說明

World Enterprise asks to be the exclusive agency for the particular product of Best Corp.

世界企業向倍斯特公司請求作為其特定產品獨家代理。

★角色介紹

（買方）Buyer: World Enterprises

（賣方）Seller: Best International Trade Corp.

情境對話

W: Mr. Yang, per your product presentation last week, we expressed high interest in your balancing valve and discussed the opportunity of becoming your exclusive agent in EU market.

W: 楊先生，從上週的產品簡報，我司表達對貴司平衡閥的高度興趣，並討論了成為貴司在歐盟市場之獨家代理商的機會。

B: That's right. We've had some preliminary discussions last week.

B: 沒錯。我們在上週有了初步的討論。

W: World Enterprise is a big industrial company in Europe, and has a history

W: 有著百年以上歷史的世界企業是歐洲大型的工

of over 100 years. As your exclusive agent, your product must reach the greatest degree of sales growth and market penetration in our local market.

業公司。成為貴司的獨家代理，貴司的產品必能在我們當地市場達到最大銷售額增長及市場滲透率。

B: Yes, we are aware of that and think that is to our advantage to open up new market in EU area.

B: 是的。我們瞭解這點，並認為這有利於我們在歐洲開發新市場。

W:I believe both of us would be benefited from the cooperation.

W:我相信我們雙方都將藉由此次合作受益。

B: Well. Kate. I'll draft an agency agreement and e-mail a copy for your review first, and then we could set up another meeting to go over the details.

B: 那麼，凱特。我會起草一份代理合約，並將副本先電郵給您審閱。而後我們再安排另一個會議核對一下細節。

W:Excellent. I'll await your email.

W:太好了。等待您的來信。

關鍵字彙

express *(v.)* [ɪk`sprɛs] 表達、陳述

同義詞 describe, say, tell

相關詞 express concern about sth. 對某物表達關切；express emotion 抒發情感

preliminary *(a.)* [prɪ`lɪmə͵nɛrɪ] 初步的

同義詞 initiatory, initial, primary

相關詞 preliminary layout 初步藍圖；preliminary inquiry 初步詢價

exclusive agent *(ph.)* 獨家代理商

同義詞 sole agent

相關詞 exclusive authority 唯一授權；exclusive sales 獨家銷售

market penetration *(ph.)* 市場滲透率

相關詞 market share 市場佔有率

解析 市場滲透率（market penetration） 是指對於有形商品的使用者比例，亦可說是用戶滲透率或者消費者佔有率，是一個品牌或產品在市場中位置的總和。不同於市場佔有率（market share） 所指為某特定區間，一個品牌或產品的銷售額在所有該類產品中的所占比例。

advantage *(n.)* [əd`væntɪdʒ] 優勢

同義詞 benefit, gain, vantage

相關詞 competitive advantage 競爭優勢；advantages and disadvantages 優劣

agreement *(n.)* [ə`grimənt] 契約

同義詞 contract, pact, treaty

相關詞 confidentiality agreement 保密協議；agreement price 協定價格

關鍵句型

be aware of sth. 知道某事

例句說明

Our customers **are well aware of** our prices.

➡ 客戶十分瞭解我們的價格。

Be aware of the registration deadline.

➡ 注意報名截止日。

替換句型

Be conscious of the registration deadline.

to one's advantage 對某人有利

例句說明

High quality will be **to your advantage** in competition.

➡ 高品質使你有競爭優勢。

The contract works to **buyer's best advantage**.

➡ 該合約對買方最得利。

替換句型

You benefit greatly by high quality.

勵志小格言

Practical wisdom is only to be learned in the school of experience.

～ By Samuel Smiles, British writer

實用的知識只有通過親身體驗才能學到。 *～英國作家 塞繆爾*

英文書信這樣寫

Dear Mr. Wesley Yung,

The object of this letter is to express that we are eager for being your sole agent in EU market.

World Enterprises is a reliable company for rich experience in the line of the industrial part for over a hundred years. Having had a professional team of sales representatives and excellent show rooms, we hereby recommend ourselves to act as your sole agent for your balancing valve in EU market.

Enclosed is our proposal agency agreement for your reference. Please feel free to contact us for further discussion of the clauses.

Thank you for your time on reading this email. We are looking forward to your favorable reply by return.

Yours sincerely,
Scott Fuller

中文翻譯

親愛的衛斯里楊先生：

特此表達我司熱切希望成為貴司在歐盟市場的獨家代理商。

世界企業為一家信譽卓越的公司，在此行業擁有逾百年的豐富經驗。我們擁有專業的銷售團隊及一流的陳列室，在此自我推薦作為貴司平衡閥在歐盟市場的獨家代理商。

請參閱附件我司提案的代理權合約。請隨時與我們聯繫，進一步討論合約條款。

感謝您撥冗審閱此文。靜候佳音！

史考特　富勒　敬啟

知識補給

代理商的種類概述：

獨家代理商（sole agent）：指製造商在同一區域內只能授權單一代理商，但製造商本身仍可在此區域進行銷售行為。

非獨家代理（simple agent）：同一區域內可同時有多家代理商，製造商本身亦可在此區域進行銷售行為。

絕對排他代理商（exclusive agent）：指製造商在同一區域內只能授權單一代理商，且製造商本身不可在此區域進行銷售行為。

職場經驗談

簽訂代理合約之前，您應該知道的幾件事：

✔ 審慎選擇代理商，才能有效達到最大銷售利益。

✔ 分析當地市場，進行代理可行性評估。

✔ 進行損益評估，注意賠償責任歸屬問題，此將關乎雙方成本及獲利。

✔ 委請相關專業法律顧問擬定合約，並審慎評估及閱讀每項條款。

銷售的目的就是在獲利，簽署任何商業文件，務必要能以保障自身利益為原則。

菜鳥變達人

中翻英練習

1. 加強英文能力將使你在貿易領域更具競爭力。

2. 製造商意識到造成質量不良的潛在問題，並採取了全面的預防措施。

中翻英解答

1. To enhance English ability will be to your advantage in the trade area.
2. The manufacturer is aware of the potential problems causing the quality defect and has taken every precaution.

1-2 開發新客戶
New Customer Development

1-2-1 尋求合作（出口商）
Exporter Looking for Customer

★情境說明

Through ABC's recommendation, Best Corp. takes the initiative to call World Enterprise to build new business relationships.

經由ABC公司的推薦，倍斯特公司主動致電世界企業，以建立新業務關係。

★角色介紹

（買方）Buyer: World Enterprises
（賣方）Seller: Best International Trade Corp.

情境對話

B: Hello! Ms. Ryder. This is Wesley Yang, the product manager at Best Corp.

B: 您好！瑞德小姐。我是倍斯特公司的產品經理衛斯理 楊。

W:How may I help you, Mr. Yang?

W:需要什麼協助嗎？楊先生。

B: I got your company's information from ABC Co. and well know you

B: 我們透過ABC公司得知貴公司的資訊，十分瞭

want to outsource industrial valve. I'm calling to introduce our company to you.	解貴司想要外包工業閥門。
W:Please keep go on.	W:請繼續。
B: We are mainly engaged in manufacturing full range of industrial valve. Our company has an excellent reputation in the States and is the Top 5 of the largest exporters of industrial valve in Taiwan.	B: 我們主要從事生產全系列工業閥門。我司在美國市場聲譽卓越，並且在台灣是工業閥門的前五大出口商。
W:What is your company's annual sales figure last year?	W:貴司的去年年度銷售額是多少？
B: Our sales volume exceeded ten million US dollars last year.	B: 我們去年年度銷售額逾一千萬美元。
W:I see. I prefer talking face to face to talking on the phone.	W:我瞭解了。比起在電話裡交談，我更傾向面對面談。
B: No problem. We can schedule a product presentation. How about 9:00 A.M., on this Friday?	B: 沒問題。我可以安排一場產品簡報。那就本週五早上九點，如何？
W:That's nice. I expect to see you in person.	W:很好。期待見到您本人。

關鍵字彙

outsource *(v.)* [ˋaʊt sors] 委外、外包

同義詞 contract work out, farm out

相關詞 outsourcing service 外包服務；outsourcing abroad 外包國外

manufacture *(v.)* [ˏmænjəˋfæktʃɚ] 製造

同義詞 construct, fabricate, make

相關詞 manufacturing 製造業；semi-manufactured goods 半成品

full range *(ph.)* 全系列

同義詞 all serial, complete series, full spectrum

相關詞 full range of sample 全套樣品；full range of service 全方位服務

reputation *(n.)* [ˏrɛpjəˋteʃən] 聲譽

同義詞 fame, honor, name

相關詞 famous reputation 盛名；reputation risk 商譽風險

exceed *(v.)* [ɪkˋsid] 超過

同義詞 better, excel, surpass

相關詞 exceeding the budget 超出預算；exceed expectations 超出預期

product presentation *(ph.)* 產品簡報

相關詞 product demonstration 產品展示；product description 產品簡介

關鍵句型

Sb. be engaged in 從事

例句說明

Jack is engaged in retail business.

➡ 傑克經營零售生意。

We are engaged in import and export.

➡ 我們從事進出口貿易。

替換句型

We work at import and export.

prefer A to B 喜歡A更勝於B

例句說明

The manufacturer **prefers road shipment to rail shipment**.

➡ 製造商寧可選擇公路運輸更勝鐵路運輸。

Consumers **prefer high price product than low quality one**.

➡ 消費者寧可選擇高價品也不要劣質品。

替換句型

Consumer would rather choose high price product than low quality one.

勵志小格言

He who does not gain loses.

學如逆水行舟，不進則退。學如逆水行舟，不進則退。

解析：比喻為學艱難。用以告誡學習應抱著嚴謹、持恆的態度，不可輕忽怠慢。

英文書信這樣寫

Dear Ms. Ryder,

Good morning! It is our highly pleasure to learn your honored name through ABC Co, and know that you are looking for industrial valve.

Please allow me to take this opportunity to introduce ourselves - Best Group. - TOP manufacturer and exporter of industrial valves with the leading manufacturing capabilities in Taiwan. Our business involves manufacture, quality inspection, foreign trade, storage, and logistics. We can provide high-quality service and credible quality to the clients all over the world. Our products mainly focus on industrial valves, such as all kinds of heating valves, check & foot valves, BS standard valves, globe valves and so on. Especially we can provide customized R&D services, according to your drawings /samples to meet your special requirements. Please visit our website www.best.com.tw to know details of our company and the full range of our product.

Thanks for your valuable time to read this letter, and we are looking forward to establishing a long-term & mutual beneficial partnership with you in the near future.

Thanks & best regards,
Wesley Yang
Product Manager
Best International Trade Corp.
Tel: 886-2-22335555 / Mobile: 886-958-223355

中文翻譯

瑞德小姐您好，

日安！我司非常榮幸透過ABC公司的介紹得知貴司的尊名，並知道貴司正在尋找工業閥門。

請容許我借此機會介紹我司 – 倍斯特集團 - 台灣具備領先工業閥門製造能力的頂尖製造商及出口廠商。我們的業務涉及製造、品質檢驗、對外貿易，以及倉儲物流。我們可以提供世界各地的客戶高品質的服務及可靠質量的產品。產品主要集中於工業閥門：如各種供暖閥門，檢查底閥，BS標準閥，截止閥等。特別是我們可以依據您的圖紙或樣品，提供客製化的研發服務來滿足您的特殊要求。請瀏覽我司的網站www.best.com.tw，以瞭解詳細公司資訊和全面的產品細節。

感謝您撥冗閱讀此封郵件，我司期待在不久的將來與貴司建立長期互惠互利的合作夥伴關係。

衛斯理　楊　敬啟
倍斯特國際貿易公司　產品經理
電話：886-2-22335555
手機：886-958-223355

知識補給

開發信書寫要點：主旨（Subject） – 具吸引力，能誘使收件者閱讀；開頭語（Opening） – 告知得知對方訊息的來源為何；本文（Body） – 精要介紹公司優勢及產品特色，不足處以附件或公司網頁做為補充；結束語（Concluding） – 表達感激受文者審閱信文及期待合作；簽名（Signature） - 在署明後加上職稱、地址、電話、傳真、電郵或手機等。

職場經驗談

開發信即為推銷信，經常被視為垃圾郵件，直接被刪除，因此主旨能引起收件者好奇心，誘使其閱讀則為重要關鍵，若能確認受文者姓名，則可直接在主旨加上受文者姓名，至少可爭取到被受文者讀取的機會。而客製化開發信勝於制式化開發信，了解單一客戶的公司背景、市場屬性及需求產品，才能正中下懷。例如：「To John Lee」、「The Supplier of Apple Inc. - Best International Trade Corp.」、「Are you satisfied with your supplier?」。

菜鳥變達人

中翻英練習

1. 至少有上千家企業參加這次展覽。

2. 經理認為我的提案勝於妮娜的，因為他覺得我的提案更有利。

中翻英解答

1. At least thousands of companies are engaged in the exhibition.
2. The manager prefers my proposal than Nina's, in that he think it is more profitable.

1-2-2 公司介紹 I
Company Profile I

★情境說明

Best Corp. makes company profile to ABC Co.
倍斯特公司向ABC公司做公司簡介

★角色介紹

（買方）Buyer: Buyer: ABC Co., Ltd.
（賣方）Seller: Seller: Best International Trade Corp.

情境對話

B: Good morning, ladies and gentlemen. On behalf of Best Group, I'd like to extend greeting to all of you, our distinguished guests, being here today. My name is Wesley Yang, product manager of Sales Department. It's our great honor to welcome your visitation.

B: 各位先生女士，早安！在此我謹代表倍斯特集團問候在座的各位嘉賓今日都能來到這裡。我是衛斯理 楊，銷售部產品經理。我們萬分榮幸歡迎諸位的蒞臨。

As many of you may know, Best Industrial was established in 1979. The factory is located in Taichung, Taiwan, mainly dealing in industrial valve manufacturing. We set up

在座諸位大多知道，倍斯特工業成立於西元1979年。本廠座落在臺灣台中市，主要從事工業閥門製造。我們設立

Business Department and formed Best International Trade Corp. in 2000. Best group has been striving to establish the market field about industrial valve all over the world.

了業務部，並在西元2000年成立倍斯特國際貿易有限公司。倍斯特一直努力在世界各地建立工業閥門的市場領域。

Please allow me to brief you about our company by the video. I'll be glad to answer all of your questions at the end.

請容許我藉由視頻向各位介紹倍斯特公司。我將樂於在簡報結束後回答諸位的提問。

after 15-minute video time...

經過15分鐘的視頻時間…

B: Thanks for your time on the video. Has anyone got any question?

B: 感謝各位的時間觀賞視頻。有人要提出任何問題嗎？

A: Please tell us about your future plan. Do you have any plan of company expansion, such as investing a new plant?

A: 請說明一下貴司的未來展望。公司是否有擴展計劃，例如投資新廠房？

B: Thank you for bring that question up. As shown on the video, our headquarter is located in Taipei, Taiwan. We have 3 branches respectively in Central, Hong Kong, the financial center, Shanghai,

B: 感謝您提出這個問題。如視頻所介紹，我們的總部設在臺灣臺北，另有3家分公司分別在亞洲金融中心之稱的香港中環、中國的上海，以及

Mainland China, and Detroit, Michigan. Another new UK office is under construction to service local customer continuously increased, and is expected to be completed by the end March of next year.

美國密西根州的底特律。另外在英國的一個新辦事處正在興建中，預計明年三月前完工，來服務當地持續增長的客戶。

A: How many people do you employ?

A: 貴司員工數是多少？

B: We have around 1,500 employees worldwide. Predicting by the end of 2015, the staff numbers will attain the scale of 2000 people, in response to company development and production needs.

B: 全球共有1500位職工。預計至2015年底，職員工人數將達到2000人的規模，以因應公司成長及生產需求。

A: What's your sales volume?

A: 貴司的銷售額為何？

B: Our worldwide sales reached 2 billion US dollar last year. Our goal for this year is the growth of 15%.

B: 我們全球銷售額在上個年度已達二十億美元。今年的目標是成長十五個百分點。

If there is no more question, keeping this chance, we are just preparing to show some prototype samples designed by Best R & D team. All of those first-hand information is really the best reference for you need.

如果沒有其他問題，藉此機會，我們準備了一些由倍斯特研發團隊設計出的原型樣品。所有這些一手資訊是因應您需求的最佳參考。

關鍵字彙

deal in *(ph.)* 經營

同義詞 do business in, trade in

相關詞 deal in product development 致力於產品開發；deal in exports 經營出口

headquarter *(n.)* 總部

同義詞 head office, main office, home base

相關詞 subsidiary company 子公司；parent company 母公司

financial center *(ph.)* 金融中心

同義詞 banking center

解析 金融中心指中心商務區，一個地區的金融首都。

關鍵句型

in response to… 因應…

例句說明

The project is to enhance product quality, **in response to** the challenge of foreign competition.

➡ 此專案的目的在於加強產品質量，以因應國外競爭者的挑戰。

We accept the goods return **in response to** customer's complaint.

➡ 我們因客訴而接受退貨。

替換句型

We accept the goods return in answer to customer's complaint.

勵志小格言

Don't be afraid to start over. It's a new chance to rebuild what you want.

~ *From www.livelifehappy.com*

不要害怕開始。這是一個新的機會來重建你想要的。

~ *摘錄至網頁 www.livelifehappy.com*

知識補給

公司簡介的內容應包含公司介紹、歷史沿革、經營理念、產品類別、生產能力、公司據點、經合格認證的證書，以及未來展望等。一般而言，經營規模較大的公司會錄製DVD動態影片檔。而中小型企業多以PowerPoint簡報為主，即便如此，簡報製作時以公司標誌為底，統一簡報格式，加入圖表及照片等作詳細介紹，亦可適時加入背景音樂，來增加簡報的生動程度。而公司簡介的內容以10 ～ 20分鐘時間較為適切。

由於網際網路的普及使用，不論規模大小的公司，絕大多數皆有屬於自己的網頁，而公司網頁內容不外乎就是公司概要。因此客戶來訪時的公司簡介內容以網站內容為主軸加以延伸，提供來訪客戶更深入且具體的介紹，尤其可著重在說明公司未來規劃、宣揚製程能力、介紹產品優勢，及實際展示現品等，來吸引客戶採購及穩固長期合作關係。

職場經驗談

貿易事務的商務拜訪以銷售或採購部門人員為主，有時會有產品設計部門或工程部門人員隨行，因此接待人員除了業務單位的負責業務或研發單位人員，最高層級大多為所屬單位的最高主管，如業務經理、協理或總經理。若來訪者為最高層級，如董事長或執行長等，則受訪者應安排對等的層級接待，以表敬意及誠意。

菜鳥變達人

中翻英練習

1. 我們不能再任由新人犯錯了。

---

2. 因應新進人員的速成訓練而召開了這次會議。

中翻英解答

1 We shouldn't allow the new staff to make mistakes any more.

2 The meeting was called in response to the quick training for new staff.

1-2-3 公司介紹 II
Company Profile II

公司簡介這樣寫

Company Profile Overview

公司簡介概要

Best Group Introduction

To cope with the fast-changing market demands, BEST Group not only has its own professional manufacturing capabilities, but also provides customized R&D services to its customers. It provides timely and complete services to its customers, showing its excellent competitiveness among other companies.

倍斯特集團簡介

現今快速變化的市場需求中，倍斯特公司除了擁有專業的製造能力外；亦可以依客戶之需求從事設計與開發，隨時提供客戶即時完整的服務，突顯出在同業間優異的競爭力。

Philosophy of Business

Best Group practices FIVE roots of BEST: Excellence in Performance, Reliability of Quality, Puncture Delivery, Fast Service, and More Income than Expenditure.

經營理念

倍斯特集團執行五大根本力：
「性能優越，品質可靠，交貨準時，服務快速，收入大於支出。」

<u>In-time Delivery System</u>

With the full command of the

<u>即時交貨系統</u>

充份掌握市場供需變化，與客戶密

changes in the market and close cooperation with the customer, and through our reserve stock system, we have sufficient corresponding capability to provide fast and exact delivery of our products.

切配合，透過平時的儲備料系統，使我們擁有充足的應變能力，以達到快速準確的交貨時程。

Quality Assurance System

Customer care is our top priority and full satisfaction and trust is what we work for.

品質保証系統

顧客的完全滿意和信賴是我們努力的目標。

Our strict QA inspection processes including raw material inspection, process inspection, and test before shipping are all conducted with precision testing equipment and all follow internationally certification standards. We are proud and confident in providing all products with good quality to our customers.

從原物料入庫檢驗，製程檢驗、出貨檢驗等嚴格的品檢流程，並經過精密的儀器檢測及國際認證標準。讓我們所交付客戶的每項產品，都是優良品，更包含了我們的自信與驕傲。

History

1979 - Best Industrial was founded with the capital of NTD 30,000 and 6 employees with the annual

公司沿革

1979年 - 倍斯特工業成立，資本額新臺幣三萬、員工6名、鑄件年產量100噸。

output of 100 tons of castings.

1980 - Best invested a mold factory to customize designs of hardware molds, core molds, tooling, and cutters for customers.

1980年 - 倍斯特工業投資模具廠，代客設計製造水用五金模具、砂心模具、治具及刀具等產品。

1985 - Best industrial developed in-house manufacturing capability of sanitary hardware valves, and actively expanded exports to Southeastern Asia countries.

1985年 - 倍斯特工業發展內部生產能力，製造衛浴五金閥門，並積極擴大出口到東南亞國家

1987 - Best industrial invested a new casting factory and developed in-house manufacturing capability of steam valve to expand business in North America.

1987年 - 倍斯特工業投資新鑄造廠，開發熱氣閥產品，並擴展美加地區業務

2000 - Best industrial set up Best International Trade Corp. and established headquarters in Taipei, Taiwan.

2000年 - 倍斯特工業成立倍斯特國際貿易公司，並在臺灣臺北成立營運總部

2002 – Best Group opened a new office respectively in Central, Hong Kong in July and in Shanghai,

2002年 - 倍斯特集團分別香港中環及中國上海成立辦公室

Mainland China in December.

2010 – Best Group opened a delivery center in Detroit, Michigan to provide better service locally.

2010年 - 倍斯特集團在美國密西根州底特律開設成立發貨中心，提供更好的在地服務

Capabilities

Hardware Molds, Core Molds, Tooling and Cutters Design & Building
Brass Casting, Forging and CNC Machining
Plastic Injection
2nd machining, Grinding, Polishing
Product Functionality Testing
Product Quality Control & Assurance
Storage & Logistics Management

生產能力

五金模具、芯模、模具和刀具的設計與建造
黃銅鑄造、鍛造、及中心加工
塑膠射出
二次加工、研磨、拋光
產品功能測試
產品品質控制和保證
倉儲物流管理

Products

Heating Valves
Check & Foot valves
BS Standard Valves
Globe valves

產品種類

供暖閥門
檢查底閥
BS標準閥
截止閥

Worldwide Locations

Headquarter - Best International Trade Corp. in Taipei Taiwan
10F.-2, No.1, Fuzhou St., Zhongzheng Dist., Taipei City, Taiwan 10078
Tel: 886-2-2351-1111 /
Fax: 886-4-2351-2222
Email: best.headquarter@best.com.tw

Taiwan Plant - Best Industrial in Taichung Taiwan
No.1, Aly. 1, Ln. 1, Gongye 1st Rd., Dali Dist., Taichung City, Taiwan 41280
Tel: 886-2-2359-1111 /
Fax: 886-4-2359-2222
Email: best.industrial@best.com.tw

Main Office - Best Corp. in Central, Hong Kong
1 Queen' s Road Central, Hong Kong
Tel: 852-222-11111 /
Fax: 852-222-22222
Email: best.hkoffice@best.com

各地據點

集團總部 -倍斯特國際貿易公司，位於臺灣臺北
10078臺灣臺北市中正區福州街1號10樓之2
電話: 886-2-2351-1111 /
傳真: 886-4-2351-2222
電郵: best.headquarter@best.com.tw

臺灣廠 - 倍斯特工業，位於臺灣臺中
41280臺灣臺中市大里區工業一路一巷一弄一號
電話: 886-2-2359-1111 /
傳真: 886-4-2359-2222
電郵: Best.industrial@best.com.tw

辦公室 - 倍斯特公司，位於香港中環
香港中環皇后大道中一號
電話: 852-222-11111 /
傳真: 852-222-22222
電郵: best.hkoffice@best.com

Main Office - Best Corp. in Shanghai, Mainland China
1 Nanjing Road East Shanghai, Shanghai 200001, China
Tel: 86-21-1111-1111 /
Fax: 86-21-2222-2222
Email: best.shoffice@best.com

辦公室 - 倍斯特公司，位於中國上海
中國上海，上海南京東路1號，郵遞區號 200001
電話: 86-21-1111-1111 /
傳真: 86-21-2222-2222
電郵: best.shoffice@best.com

Delivery Center - Best Inc. in Detroit, Michigan USA
1111 East Jefferson Avenue, Detroit, MI 48204, USA
Tel: 734-111-1111 /
Fax: 734-222-2222
Email: best.micenter@best.com

發貨中心 - 倍斯特公司，美國密西根州的底特律
美國密西根州底特律市傑弗遜東道1111號，郵遞區號48204
電話: 734-111-1111 /
傳真: 734-222-2222
電郵: best.micenter@best.com

1-2-4 產品介紹（對首次見面客戶）
Product Introduction to New Customer

★情境說明

Best Corp. introduces product to new customer.
倍斯特公司向新客戶介紹產品

★角色介紹

（新客戶）Customer: Victor Ltda.
（賣　方）Seller: Best International Trade Corp.

情境對話

B: Our product range includes industrial valve in three main material, brass, bronze, and low-lead. We're one of the major manufacturers in Taiwan, and the second largest supplier in the world.

I'd like to introduce you these items, our best-selling products: gate valve, globe valve, and check valve. They all have quality assurance specifications ISO9001 certification and sell very fast every year.

B: 我們的產品種類主要為三大類材質的工業閥門，銅、黃銅以及低鉛銅。我們是台灣區主要的製造商之一，並且為全球第二大供應商。

我想向您介紹這些項目，我們最暢銷的產品：閘閥，截止閥，止回閥。它們都有品質保證規範，ISO9001認證。這些產品每年有很大的銷售量。

V: How about your market share?

B: We have a very large market share in the States and has achieved above 20% last quarter. We hope our new product range will increase our market share next year.

V: Do you have the plan of developing new market?

B: We're now actively expanding abroad market to establish a long-term cooperation partnership, especially for EU area. We believe we can successfully challenge for market share there.

V: Talking about your inspection system.

B: The factory is equipped with complete hydraulic, pressure inspection equipment, to achieve the shipment of one hundred percent inspection, and to provide customers with the highest quality products.

V: 你們的市場佔有率如何?

B: 我們在美國地區有很大的市場佔有率，上一季已超過20%。希望下一個年度我們的新系列能增加我們的市場佔有量。

V: 貴司有開發新市場的計畫嗎?

B: 我們正積極拓展國外市場，以建立長期合作夥伴關係，尤其針對歐盟市場。相信我們能夠成功爭取到該區的市場佔有率。

V: 談談貴司的品檢系統。

B: 本廠配備完整的液壓，壓力檢測設備等，以達到百分百出貨檢驗，為客戶提供最高品質的產品。

關鍵字彙

best-selling *(a.)* 最暢銷

同義詞 number-one-selling, most popular

相關詞 selling point 賣點；selling agent 銷售代理

market share *(ph.)* 市場佔有率

相關詞 market size forecasting 市場規模預測

解析 市場佔有率所指為某特定區間，一個品牌或產品的銷售額在所有該類產品中的所占比例

major *(a.)* [`medʒɚ] 主要的

同義詞 main, primary, principal

相關詞 major premise 大前提；major-league 第一流的

product range *(ph.)* 產品種類

同義詞 product type, product category

相關詞 product line 生產線；product introduction 產品介紹

expand *(v.)* [ɪk`spænd] 擴展

同義詞 extend, spread

相關詞 expand the factory 擴大工廠；expand production 擴大生產

establish *(v.)* [ə`stæblɪʃ] 建立

同義詞 build, set up

相關詞 pre-establish 預定；re-establish 重建

關鍵句型

I'd like to introduce… 我想介紹…

例句說明

I'd like to introduce you to our CEO.

➡ 我想介紹你認識我們的執行長。

I'd like to introduce myself to you.

➡ 我想向你作自我介紹。

替換句型

Allow me to present my CEO to you.

Sb. successfully challenge for… 成功挑戰…

例句說明

I successfully challenged for the project award.

➡ 我成功爭取到此專案。

He successfully challenged for the chief salesman.

➡ 他成功成為首席業務。

替換句型

I succeed in getting the project award.

英文書信這樣寫

Dear Mr. Nate,

We are very pleased to receive your call, knowing that you are interested in our products.

Let us introduce ourselves as a manufacturer and exporter, establishing a good reputation in the field of industrial valves at home and abroad. We can provide customers around the world with high quality service and reliable quality, in fields covering manufacturing, quality inspection, foreign trade, warehousing, and logistics field.

Over the years, our company set up a complete set of product system, containing a variety of heating valves, check valve, BS standard valve, and cut-off valve. Please see the attachment for the latest catalogue and price list.

We believe our professional technology and quality inspection system will bring us a win-win situation. In addition, it is worth mentioning that, we can provide you with a competitive price.

Looking forward to receiving a favorable reply soon.

Thanks & best regards,
Wesley Yang
Product Manager
Best International Trade Corp.
Tel:886-2-22335555 / Mobile:886-958-223355

中文翻譯

奈特先生您好，

很高興接到您的來電，得知貴司對我們的產品感興趣。

請容在下介紹我司，為在國內和國外工業閥門領域建立了良好的信譽製造商及出口商。我們可以提供世界各地的客戶，高品質的服務和可靠的品質，涵蓋生產製造，品質檢驗，對外貿易，倉儲物流等領域。

多年來，我司已擁有一套完整的產品體系，包含各種供暖閥門，檢查底閥，BS標準閥，截止閥等。請參閱附件最新的產品目錄及報價表。

相信我司的專業技能及品檢系統會為我們帶來雙贏局面。此外，值得一提的是，我們可以為您提供具有競爭力的價格。

靜候佳音！

衛斯理　楊　敬啟
產品經理
倍斯特國際貿易公司
電話：886-2-22335555
手機：886-958-223355

知識補給

如何善用網際網路開發業務? 關於業務開發，在前面章節中提到了參加商展，藉以增加產品的曝光率，吸引國外訪客。除此之外，也要把握商展網頁提供的資料，一般大型會展網頁上會列載展商的聯絡資料及經營產品項目，國外的展商也可能是潛在的客戶，可以主動發送開發信介紹產品。另外，可利用各國網路黃頁以及搜尋引擎交叉查詢同業客戶資料，這些可都是免費的資源喔! 黃頁網站例舉如下：

美國黃頁www.superpages.com
歐洲黃頁www.europages.com
澳洲黃頁www.yellowpages.com.au
大中華黃頁貿易網www.hiyp.com.tw

職場經驗談

對於未合作過的新客戶提出需求時，不同於對既有客戶著重在詳述特定產品規格，可藉此介紹公司服務項目及優勢，強調生產技術、品質系統及價格條件等吸引客戶，開啟首次合作的契機。

勵志小格言

Fortune does favor the bold and you'll never know what you're capable of if you don't try.
~ Sheryl Sandberg, Chief Operating Officer of Facebook

運氣的確是眷顧有勇氣的人，你如果不嘗試，你永遠不知道你能完成什麼。
～臉書營運長　雪莉　桑德伯格

菜鳥變達人

中翻英練習

1. 我想把凱特介紹給我們的一些主要職員。

2. 已成功達到百分之百準時出貨率。

中翻英解答

1 I'd like to introduce Kate to some of our key personnel.
2 It has been successfully challenged for 100% on-time delivery rate.

1-2-5 信用調查
Credit Investigation

★情境說明

Best Corp. makes credit-counseling with ABC Co.
倍斯特公司向ABC公司提出信用諮詢。

★角色介紹

（買方）Buyer: ABC Co., Ltd.
（賣方）Seller: Best International Trade Corp.

情境對話

B: Good afternoon. This is Wesley Yang calling form Best Corp. I'm calling for Olivia.

B: 下午好。我是倍斯特公司的衛斯理 楊，我找奧利維亞。

A: Olivia is on the line. Please go ahead.

A: 我是奧利維亞，請說。

B: I'd request you to do me a favor. A firm named Great Inc. described themselves as one of the TOP major importers in your local area send an inquiry to us. We tried to locate this company in vain, and hesitate to take their inquiry.

B: 請您幫我一個忙。一家名叫偉大股份有限公司聲稱自己為你們所在地區最主要的進口商之一，發詢盤給我們。我們試圖找這家公司的紀錄，但徒勞無功，因此猶豫是否承接他們的詢價。

A: Oh! We have had dealings with them several years ago.

A: 哦！我們幾年前與他們打過交道。

B: It seems that I come to the right person. Could you share with me some information about their credibility, financial condition, and trade contacts?

B: 看來我找對人了。您能與我分享一些有關他們的信用能力、財務狀況及貿易往來狀況的相關訊息嗎？

A: It's the unpleasant experience of doing business with them. The alarmingly high turnover and quality of staff seriously affect the work efficiency.

A: 與他們做生意是很不愉快的經歷。令人擔憂的高員工流動率以及員工素質嚴重影響工作效率。

B: Do you have any idea why they turn to other supplier rather than the original sources?

B: 你知道為什麼他們轉向其他的供應商，而不是原始的供貨來源嗎？

A: Credit fraud and default should be the biggest problems. We have stopped deliveries, because they fall into arrears with our bill.

A: 信用欺詐和違約應該是最大的問題。我們已經停止供貨，因為他們拖欠我們的帳款。

B: It's too terrible. Appreciate for your kind sharing. Please be assured that your information will be kept confidential in strict.

B: 真是太糟糕了。感謝你的分享。請放心，您的資訊將會嚴格保密。

關鍵字彙

dealings *(n.)* [ˋdilɪŋs] **交易；商業往來**

同義詞 business transaction, business deal

相關詞 financial dealings金融交易；questionable dealings 不誠實的交易

credibility *(n.)* [ˏkrɛdəˋbɪlətɪ] **信用能力**

同義詞 trustworthiness, dependability

相關詞 credibility crisis 信任危機；credibility problem 信譽問題

trade contacts *(ph.)* **貿易往來**

同義詞 trade exchanges, trade dealings

相關詞 global trade 世界貿易；bilateral trade 雙邊貿易

turnover *(n.)* [ˋtɝnˏovɚ] **流動；周轉**

同義詞 change, reversal (of money, goods, people)

相關詞 inventory turnover 存貨周轉；turnover of trade 貿易流通量

fraud *(n.)* [frɔd] **欺騙；詭計**

同義詞 cheating, deceit, swindle

相關詞 business fraud 商業詐騙；fraud charge 詐欺罪

default *(n.)* [dɪˋfɔlt] **拖欠；違約**

同義詞 nonpayment, failure to pay on time

相關詞 default fine 過期罰金；default clause 違約條款

關鍵句型

fall into arrears with 拖欠

例句說明

The pledged realty has been expropriated, as your company **fell into arrears with** the loan

➡ 因貴司拖欠貸款，貴司抵押之不動產已被沒收。

Your company **have fallen into arrears with** three-month's rent.

➡ 貴司已拖欠三個月租金。

替換句型

Your company have fallen behind with three-month's rent.

be assured that… 放心…

例句說明

How can we **be assured that** the shipment have been fully inspected?

➡ 我們怎麼能確信該批貨經過完整檢驗?

You can **be assured that** the shipment passed 100% inspection.

➡ 你放心，這筆貨通過百分百全檢合格。

替換句型

You can set your mind at rest that the shipment passed 100% inspection.

勵志小格言

If you live each day as if it was your last, someday you'll most certainly be right.

~ Steve Jobs

如果你把每天都當成最後一天來過，總有一天你會證明自己是對的。

～蘋果公司創辦人　賈伯斯

英文書信這樣寫

Dear Sir,

Great Inc. with details under-mentioned recently approached us for having business dealings with us and referred us to your bank.

We shall appreciate your bank to provide us with related information of their financial and business status, and meet all the expenses incurred in this connection upon being notified.

Please accept our apology for any trouble and inconvenience we may cause you. You may rest assured that any information provided will be conducted entirely in confidential, without responsibility on your party.

Yours sincerely,
Wesley Yang

中文翻譯

敬啟者：

偉大股份有限公司近期與我司接洽業務往來事宜，並向我司推薦貴行進行諮詢。

我司感謝貴行能提供有關偉大公司的財務和業務狀況的相關資訊，在被告知之情形下，我司將負擔所有因此產生之費用。

對於可能帶來貴行任何麻煩和不便，請接受我司的歉意。請放心，貴行提供的任何資訊將完全保密，你方不負任何責任。

衛斯理　楊　敬啟

知識補給

信用調查（Credit Investigation）或稱為徵信，簡而言之是對個人或企業進行信用驗證，可透過雙方往來銀行、國內外資信業者或我方同行合作夥伴協助進行。調查的內容較常依據的架構有兩大類：

1. 5C：品格（Character）、能力（Capacity）、資本（Capital）、擔保品（Collateral）、經營條件（Condition）。
2. 5P：借款戶因素（People）、資金用途因素（Purpose）、還款財源因素（Payment）、債權保障因素（Protection）、授信展望因素（Perspective）。

信用調查的簡要流程：選擇調查機構／調查方式 → 確認調查內容 → 開始進行調查 → 整理調查結果 → 撰寫調查報告 → 提供調查報告

（以上內容參考：MBA 智庫 & 維京百科 網站）

職場經驗談

企業間在進行交易前進行徵信極為重要，尤其是針對新客戶、久未往來之客戶及位於政治環境動盪國家之客戶等。信用調查的內容主要針對財務條件、信用狀況及經營能力等方面進行調查，調查的目的無非就是為了避免買賣雙方交易後無法獲得應有利益。

選擇的信用調查機構如果是金融業者，最好是行庫對行庫，例如我方往來銀行向對方往來銀行提出，不論是透過哪一個信用調查機構，都須提供給調查機構有關授信者的完整公司名稱及住址，以及其往來行庫名稱與帳號等。我方在正式啟動交易前，可向對方要求提供上述資料，而一般信譽良好的企業甚至會主動提供相關資料。

菜鳥變達人

中翻英練習

1. 進口商拖欠銀行利息。

---

2. 向銀行保證三天內付息。

中翻英解答

1 The importer fell into arrears with bank interests.

2 The bank is assured that the interests will be paid within three days.

1-3 新產品開發
New Product Development

1-3-1 產品評估
Product Evaluation

★情境說明

ABC Co. requests Best Corp. for new product evaluation.
ABC公司要求倍斯特公司進行新產品評估。

★角色介紹

（買方）Buyer: ABC Co., Ltd.
（賣方）Seller: Best International Trade Corp.

情境對話

A: Hey Wesley. It's Olivia calling. Would you have a moment to talk about our new RFQ?

A: 嘿，衛斯理。我是奧利維亞。你有時間來談談我們的新報價嗎？

B: Sure. The inquiry and part drawing are under evaluation. Is there anything we need to pay particular attention to while evaluating?

B: 當然。詢價單和產品圖現正在評估中。我們有什麼需要特別注意的評價？

A: Yes, please quote based on EAU 100K and 200K respectively. Sorry for not remarking it on the RFQ sheet in advance.

A: 是的，報價請分別以100K及200K為基礎。抱歉未事先在詢價單中備註。

B: Never mind. It's not a big deal. Anything else?

B: 沒關係。這不是大問題。還有要注意的嗎？

A: It's obvious that we barely have time to approve the part by next ISH show. Will your team be able to finish the cosmetic sample firstly one month earlier than ISH show date?

A: 很明顯地來不及在ISH展前核可樣品。您的團隊是否能夠在ISH展日的前一個月先完成外觀樣品呢？

B: Well. As you know, it would take 3 weeks for tool building plus 10 days for sampling at least. If there is only 3 weeks for us to complete the samples based on your timeframe, we'll be cutting it too fine.

B: 嗯…你知道，模具建構至少三週，加上打樣至少要十天。如果基於您時間範圍，只允許三週完成樣品，我們的時間就卡得太緊了。

A: I know this is a difficult request and imposition.

A: 我知道這是一個強人所難的要求。

B: How about having the cosmetic samples delivered to ISH hall directly, so that we can save the shipping time for the sample preparation?

B: 不如直接把外觀樣品寄到ISH展館，這樣我們可以節省運輸時間來做樣品製備？

A: It should be feasible.

A: 這樣應該可行。

關鍵字彙

remark *(v.)* [rɪ`mɑrk] **談到，評論**

同義詞 state, make mention of, write comment on

相關詞 meaning of the remark 這個說法的義涵

not a big deal *(ph.)* [nɒt ə big di:l] **沒什麼大不了的**

同義詞 no big deal, noting very important, not a critical

相關詞 Big deal ! (反話) 有什麼了不起；so what? 那又怎樣

barely *(adv.)* [ˈbeəli] **勉強，幾乎沒有**

同義詞 hard, just, merely

相關詞 barely alive 奄奄一息；barely enough 將就

timeframe *(n.)* [taɪmfreɪm] **時間範圍**

同義詞 period of time, time frame, time range

相關詞 any timeframe 任何時間週期；assessment timeframe 評估週期

cut it fine *(ph.)* [kʌt it fain] **時間卡得緊**

同義詞 it is too rush, it is too tight

反義詞 take one's time, not to hurry

imposition *(n.)* [ˌɪmpə`zɪʃən] **強制，強加**

同義詞 burdensome requirement, act of compelling

相關詞 imposition of duties 關稅課徵；severe impositions 嚴格要求

關鍵句型

Sb. need to pay particular attention to sth. 某人需特別關注某事

例句說明

The engineer needs to pay particular attention to the tooling building status to ensure submission on time.

➡ 工程師需特別注意模具建構情形，以確保準時送樣。

Buyers needs to pay particular attention to the material cost, so that they can request cost reduction from sellers accordingly.

➡ 買方需特別注意原物料價格，才能依此要求賣方降價。

替換句型

Obviously, the material costs are the key point that the buyers will focus on when raise up the proposal of cost reduction to sellers.

There is barely time to V 來不及做某事

例句說明

There is barely time to request sellers to revise the piece price based on the updated material cost.

➡ 來不及要求賣方依據最新原物料價格修改產品單價。

There is barely time to implement 100% inspection before release.

➡ 沒有足夠的時間在出貨前進行全檢。

替換句型

It's too late to implement 100% inspection before release.

英文書信這樣寫

Dear Olivia,

We have duly received your inquiry of your part number A5197 by email dated Jan. 10th, and took the liberty to enclose the quotation sheet herein. Meanwhile, you may refer to our proposal engineering suggestions as the drawings attached.

If there's no further comment, please revise our engineering drawing per our proposal by return and release the tooling as well as sample order to kick off tooling building and sample preparation. Or else, please share your concern for our reference.

We hope to receive your reply without any delay to kick off new product development immediately to meet your urgent demand.

Yours sincerely,
Wesley Yang

中文翻譯

奧莉維亞您好：

我們已正式透過貴司一月十日的電郵收到貴司編號A5197的詢價，在此提供附件報價單。同時，貴司可以參考我司建議的工程建議如附圖。

如果貴司無進一步的評論，請依據我司工程建議改回圖紙並下模具及樣品訂單，以啟動模具製造和樣品製備。否則，請提供您的考量點供我司參考。

我司期盼收到您立即的回覆，並即刻啟動新產品開發來因應貴司急迫的需求。

衛斯理　楊　敬啟

勵志小格言

If you can dream it, you can do it.

~ By Walt Disney

如果你有夢想，你就可以做到。

～華特・迪士尼

知識補給

OEM（Original Equipment Manufacturer 原始設備製造商）：

OEM 是指由買方或進口商提供產品品牌及設計，授權賣方或製造商依據其產品設計進行生產，再由買方或進口商進行後續銷售。OEM 的商業模式開始新興於未開發或開發中人力成本較低的國家，主要是對於勞力密集業的產品可大大降生產成本，亞洲區的日本、台灣、大陸及印度在經濟發展初期即是以 OEM 為主要商業模式，然而隨著經濟起飛，導致通貨膨脹等等環境及經濟因素，這樣的「代工」生產模式已不敷經濟成本效益，因此買方也逐漸轉移陣地尋找其它低人力成本之生產國，而原本以OEM為主的國家也試圖轉型，開發自有品牌，設計及行銷自家產品，或包辦研發及設計，最後以它牌名稱代理銷售等，即所謂的ODM（Original Design Manufacture）原始設計製造。

職場經驗談

以作者實務經驗，大陸或台灣地區現行的OEM 生產流程大致如下：

1. 買方（或進口商）提供產品設計圖予賣方（或製造商）進行評估 →
2. 賣方（或製造商）評估產品生產可行性，並提供修改建議及報價予買方（或進口商）審核 →
3. 買賣雙方確認最終產品設計圖及產品價格 →
4. 賣方（或製造商）進行產品打樣，並提樣予買方（或進口商）審核，即所謂的 PPAP（Production Part Approval Process）
5. 買方（或進口商）審核通過樣品（PPAP Approval）→
6. 賣方（或製造商）進行量產（mass production）出貨予買方（或進口商）進行銷售。

菜鳥變達人

1. 提供報價單前你需特別留意各個金額。

2. 即使沒有足夠的時間逐一檢視報價單上的產品單價，但你需盡你所能。

中翻英解答

1 You need to pay particular attention to each dollar sign before offer.

2 Even though there is barely time to check the piece price one by one on the sheet, you must do your best.

1-3-2 產品開發
Product Development

★情境說明

ABC Co. awards Best Corp. new product development.
ABC公司授予倍斯特公司進行新產品開發。

★角色介紹

（買方）Buyer: ABC Co., Ltd.
（賣方）Seller: Best International Trade Corp.

情境對話

A: This is Olivia Porter from ABC Co. I'd like to talk to Wesley Yang. Could you please put me through?

A: 我是ABC公司的奧利維亞波特。我想找衛斯理楊，麻煩您？

B: Hang on a second. I'll connect you now.

B: 請稍待。我現在為您轉接。

B: This is Wesley speaking.

B: 我是衛斯理。

A: Hello, Wesley, this is Olivia. I'm calling to tell you that the drawing of our part number A5197 was revised per your engineering proposal, except

A: 您好！衛斯理。我是奧利維亞。我打電話是要告知您我司產品編號A5197的圖紙已依貴司

dimension 2.50. This is critical dimension and must be kept within +0.05/-0.25 at least.

的工程方案修改，除了尺寸2.50。這是個關鍵尺寸，必須至少維持在+0.05/-0.25內。

B: Let me repeat the required tolerance just to make sure. The required tolerance is +0.05/-0.25. That means the dimension should be within 2.25 to 2.55.

B: 讓我重複一遍公差要求來確認。所需的公差為+0.05/-0.25。這意味著該尺寸應在2.25到2.55區間。

A: Completely correct.

A: 完全正確。

B: Let me check with our engineer and call you back within twenty minutes.

B: 讓我與工程師確認一下，並在二十分鐘內回電給您。

A: Thank you. If the required dimension is feasible, we can release the order to kick off tooling building today.

A: 感謝您。如果所要求的尺寸可行的話，我司可在今日內下單啟動模具製作。

關鍵字彙

award *(v.)* [ə`wɔrd] **授予、給予**

同義詞 give to, confer

相關詞 award of contract；award-winning 獲獎的；應獲獎的

put through *(ph.)* [putθru] **接通(電話)、完成(計畫)**

同義詞 transfer, connect by phone

相關詞 put through the hoop 使經歷苦難

hang on *(ph.)* [hæŋɔn] **緊抓不放、不掛斷**

同義詞 wait a minute, hold on

反義詞 hang on sb's lips 為某人的口才所迷；hang on to one's words 熱切地聽某人的話

connect *(v.)* [kə`nɛkt] **接通、連結**

同義詞 put through, link, establish communication with sb.

相關詞 connect with 與…聯繫；connect up 接通

kick off *(ph.)* [kikɔf] **開球、啟動**

同義詞 beginning action, start , commence

相關詞 kick off the party 派對開始；kick off on (date) 何日開始

關鍵句型

A take the liberty of V-ing B …

A藉此機會(冒昧地/自作主張地)對B ….

例句說明

May **I take the liberty of asking you** to provide some samples?

➡ 我可以冒昧地請您提供一些樣品嗎?

The supplier took the liberty of sending me some samples.

➡ 供應商主動寄給我一些樣品。

替換句型

The supplier took the advantage of this opportunity to send me some samples.

In accordance with the agreement contained in one's favor of (date)

依據某人某日來函同意

In accordance with the agreement contained in the buyer's favor of May 1st, the air shipment will be effected with fright collect.

➡ 依據買方五月一日來函同意，該批空運貨物將以運費到付出貨。

In accordance with the agreement contained in David's favor of May 1st, the part cost will be reduced 3% from next month.

➡ 依據大偉五月一日來函同意，產品價格將從下個月起降價3%。

替換句型

According to the agreement given in David's mail dated May 1st, the part cost will be reduced 3% from next month.

勵志小格言

We don't get a chance to do that many things, and everyone should be really excellent. ~ Steve Jobs

人這輩子沒辦法做太多事，所以每一件事情都要做到精采絕倫。

～蘋果公司創辦人 賈伯斯

英文書信這樣寫

Dear Wesley,

We take the liberty of informing you that part number A5197 is awarded to Best Co. based on your quotation sheet of Jan. 11 and the engineering proposal agreed mutually.

Enclosed please find the final 2D & 3D file, tooling order, and sample order. In accordance with the agreement contained in your favor of Jan. 12, please follow the timeframe of new product development as below.
- Estimated date of tooling completion: Feb. 2.
- Estimated date of sample completion: Feb. 12

In addition, a kick-off meeting is suggested to be held for review and discussion of proposed engineering issues to smooth the tooling building as well as sampling. We'll try to arrange a mutually convenient time and give you a notification in soon.

Any question, please let me know.

Yours sincerely,
Olivia Porter

中文翻譯

衛斯理您好：

我司通知您，產品編號A5197將依據貴司一月十一日報價表及雙方同意之工程方案，委由貴司開發生產。

隨函附上最終的2D和3D檔案、模具訂單，以及樣品訂單。依據貴司一月十二日所同意，請遵循新產品開發時程如下：

預估模具完成日：二月二日。
預估樣品完成日：二月十二日

此外，建議舉行產品啟始會議檢視及討論提出的工程議題，以使開模及打樣順利進行。我們會儘可能安排一個雙方都方便的時間，並很快的給您一個通知。

有任何問題，請讓我知道。

奧莉維亞波特　敬啟

知識補給

商用英文電話開頭語彙整篇（打招呼、表明身分、寒暄）：

1. "Hello. It's Wesley Yang Calling from Best Corp. I'd like to speak to Miss Olivia Porter, please."
2. "Hello. This is Linda Kuo calling on behalf of Mr. Wesley Yang. Is Miss Olivia Porter there, please?"
3. "Hey, Olivia. This is Wesley Yang at Best Corp."
4. "I'm looking for Miss Olivia Porter, please."
5. "May I talk to Miss Olivia Porter, please?"
6. "Could you put me through Miss Olivia Porter, please?"

職場經驗談

致電予客戶先禮貌的表明身分、問候對方，並簡單的寒暄話家常是必要的，避免劈頭談論公事。在簡單的寒暄後即可進入主題，在談話的過程中除了談論我方致電的主題外，雙方也可能隨時穿插談論其它議題，在談話的最後可做個總結，重複一次雙方談論的內容，最後則是禮貌的結束通話，例如： "It's nice to talk to you." ， "I'm looking forward to meeting you." ， "Talk to you soon. Good Luck!" ， "Appreciate. I'll let you go."

菜鳥變達人

中翻英練習

1. 部門主管主動通知新人通過試用。

2. 依據主管五月一日來函同意，報到日可延到下個月。

中翻英解答

1 The section leader takes the liberty of announcing to the new employee of his pass.

2 In accordance with the agreement contained in the leader's favor of May 1st, the on-board date can be extend to next month.

1-3-3 啟始會議
Kick-off Meeting

★情境說明

Best Corp. and ABC Co. hold kick-off video conference of new product development to review and discuss engineering issues

倍斯特公司及ABC公司舉行產品開發啟始視訊會議，檢視及討論工程議題。

★角色介紹

（買方）Buyer: ABC Co., Ltd.

（賣方）Seller: Best International Trade Corp.

情境對話

A (O): Hello, gentleman. I'm Olivia, and the guys sitting next to me is Kenny, our senior engineer, and Woody, our engineering manager.	A（O）：您好，先生們。我是奧利維亞，坐在我旁邊的是我司的高級工程師肯尼，以及我司的工程經理伍迪。
A (K & W): Hi, everyone.	A（K & W）：大家好。
B (W): Nice to meet you, Kenny and Woody. May I introduce myself Wesley Yang, product manager of Best Corp. Meanwhile, please allow	B（W）：肯尼、伍迪，很高興見到二位。自我介紹一下，我是倍斯特公司的銷售經理衛斯理

me to introduce our tooling manager Ian Chen and his team members.

楊。請允許我介紹我們的模具經理伊恩陳和他的團隊成員。

B (I & T): Hello, guys.

B（I&T）：您好，夥計們。

A (O): OK. Let's cut to the chase. I believe there is no objection of the engineering issues and it's unnecessary to go over the dimensions one by one, right?

A（O）：好吧！讓我們切入主題。我相信沒有人對工程議題有異議，不需一一檢視尺寸，對吧？

B (W): Correctly.

B（W）：正確。

A (O): Great. My engineering team would like to remind that the draft angle of tooling should be maintained as smaller as best. Further, all critical dimensions must be controlled indeed to fit with the matting parts.

A（O）：太好了。我的工程團隊要提醒的是，模具拔模角應儘量保持在越小越好。並且所有關鍵尺寸務必控制住，以能與其配合件組配。

B (I): Theirs is no problem to control the dimensions within limit in the first stage of tooling shot. However, as you know, the dimensions would fail caused by wearing, holding-on, cold

B（I）：關於這點，在模具射出的初期是沒有問題的。然而，您也知道，尺寸會因磨損、持續、冷熱疲勞等而失效，尤

and hot fatigue, and etc., especially for the part calling out limited tolerance. In this case, it would reduce the die life and tooling shot cycle.

其是對有限公差的產品。在這種情況下，它會降低模具壽命和模具射出週期。

A (O): We quite understand your meaning. Is it possible to use mold material with more wearing resistance?

A（O）：我們很理解你的意思。可以使用更耐磨模具材料嗎？

B (W): What we used is the highest quality to reduce wear and prolong die life.

B（W）：我們使用的是減少磨損及延長模具壽命的最高品質了。

A (O): I see. We don't have further engineering concern now.

A（O）：瞭解。我們沒有進一步的工程考量了。

B (W): Neither do we.

B（W）：我們也沒有。

A (O): As already mentioned, this project means a lot to ABC Co. In order to oversee the efficiency of the project operation to ensure on-time schedule, we'd suggest a weekly conference call to track the progress.

A（O）：正如已經提到的，這個專案對ABC公司來說相當重要，為了監督該項目的運行效率確保專案進度，我們建議每週電話會議來跟蹤進度。

B (W): No problem. How about every Friday morning, said 6:00 a.m. of your local time?

B（W）：沒問題。那就每個星期五的早晨，您當地時間上午六點，如何？

A (O): Agreed. By the way, my engineering manager and I may plan a visit to your plant – just in case the part can't develop smoothly.

A（O）：同意。順便說一下，我司工程經理與我可能計畫訪問貴司工廠，只是以防萬一產品無法順利發展。

B (W): Got it. Keep in touch.

B（W）：瞭解了。保持聯繫。

關鍵字彙

objection *(n.)* [əb`dʒɛkʃən] 反對、異議

同義詞 dissent, disapproval, protest

相關詞 objection overruled 反對無效；objection sustained 反對有效

fit with *(ph.)* [fitwið] 與…組配

同義詞 assemble with, meet with

相關詞 fit together 組合；fit in with 適合；fit out 配備

caused by *(ph.)* [kɔ:zd baɪ] 起因於

同義詞 result from, arise from；arise out of

相關詞 in the cause of 為了…；cause a disaster 造成災難

resistance *(n.)* [rɪˈzɪstəns] 抵抗

同義詞 opposition, act of withstanding, endurance

相關詞 resistance exercise 阻力訓練；war of resistance 抗戰

prolong *(v.)* [prə`lɔŋ] 延長、拉長

同義詞 extend, lengthen, make longer

相關詞 prolonged sound 延續的聲音

efficiency *(n.)* [ɪ`fɪʃənsɪ] 效率、功效

反義詞 inefficiency, incompetency, incapability

相關詞 market efficiency市場效率；high efficiency 高效率；high efficiency factor 高效率

關鍵句型

Let's cut to the chase. 讓我們切入主題

例句說明

As the time is limit, **let's cut to the chase**.

➡ 由於時間有限，讓我們切入主題吧!

替換句型

As the time is limit, let's get right to the point.

Sth. means a lot to Sb. 某事對某人意義重大

例句說明

Your support means a lot to us.

➡ 您的支持對我們來說意義重大。

The timely delivery means a lot to our clients, as they are almost out of stock.

➡ 準時交貨對我的客戶來說十分重要，因此他們快要斷貨了。

替換句型

The timely delivery is of great significance to our clients, as they are almost out of stock.

As the time is limit, let's come to the topic.

勵志小格言

If you think you are beaten, you are. You've got to be sure of yourself before you can ever win a prize.

~ From English Poetry of Thinking

如果你認為你被打敗了，你就是被打敗。你得在你能贏得一個獎前先肯定自己。

~ 摘錄自英文詩

知識補給

若為首次開會，會議開始先由與會雙方主席介紹與會人員，或者與會者也可進行簡單自我介紹，但人員介紹切忌冗長或過多的閒話家常，畢竟舉行專案會議的目的在於討論專案本身，再且與國外客戶開會多存在時差問題，應儘速討論要點，避免在會議中長篇大論。商務會議的精髓應在於即時切入主題，以精確執行後續工作，而身為專業的國貿從業人員應該在會議前先做足功課，才能掌握住討論要點。

職場經驗談

因應網際網路的普及應用，與國外客戶進行商務會議可說是隨時隨地可進行，小至一對一的電話會議或使用個人手提電腦進行視訊會議，大至使用專業視訊設備進行多人會議。無論使用何種方式或設備，務必將相關連線資訊、設備及會議資料等等備妥，若在雙方同意的情形下，也可先進行連線測試，使會議可順利啟動及進行。

菜鳥變達人

中翻英練習

1. 中國新年對我們來說意義重大，因為它是全家人團聚的日子。

2. 停止喃喃自語，讓我們直接切入主題吧！

中翻英解答

1. The Chinese New Year means a lot to us, as it is a reunion date for whole family.
2. Stop murmuring and let's cut to the chase.

1-3-4 會議記錄
Meeting Minutes

★情境說明

Best Corp. minutes the meeting proceedings with ABC Co. and shares the meeting minutes.

倍斯特公司記錄與ABC公司會議之事項，並提供會議紀錄。

★角色介紹

（買方）Buyer: ABC Co., Ltd.
（賣方）Seller: Best International Trade Corp.

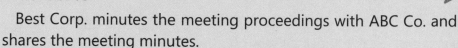

英文書信這樣寫

Dear All,

Good day!

We were pleased to have this opportunity of meeting with you guys today. You may refer to the meeting minutes as shown on the next page.

In case of any discrepancy per our discussion result, please never hesitate to let us know.

Yours sincerely,
Linda Kuo for Wesley Yang

Meeting Minutes

Meeting Date: January 13

Attendee: (Best Corp.)Wesley Yang, Ian Chen, and engineering team

(ABC Co.) Olivia Porter, Kenny, Woody

Subject: Kick-off Meeting of P/N A5197 NPD

Recorder: Linda of Best Corp.

Topic	Details
Engineering Issues	✔ Best and ABC mutually confirmed the agreed engineering suggestion without objection.
	✔ ABC team raised up the draft angle of tooling as smaller as possible. All critical dimensions related to matting dimension must be kept.
	✔ Best and ABC mutually understand the difficulty of keeping the dimensions of P/N 5197 calling out narrow tolerance range than others, even though Best already used the highest material to reduce the die wearing.
Weekly Conference	✔ The weekly conference call will be held at 6:00 a.m. (L.A. time)/ 10:00p.m. (Taiwan time) on Friday to update the NPD progress.
Other Issues	✔ Whether ABC's proposed visit to Best plant comes off will depend on parts of development progress.

中文翻譯

各位好：

我司很高興今天有機會與各位會議。請參會議記錄如下頁所示。

如與我們的討論結果有任何差異，請隨時讓我們知道。

琳達郭　代　衛斯理楊　敬啟

會議紀錄

會議日期：一月十三日

與會人員：（倍斯特公司）衛斯理楊、伊恩陳、工程組員

*（**ABC** 公司）奧莉維亞波特、肯尼、伍迪*

*討論議題： 產品編號**A5197**新產品開發啟始會議*

紀錄者：倍斯特公司　琳達

主題	細節
工程議題	✔ 倍斯特與ABC相互確認了協議的工程建議無異議。
	✔ ABC團隊提出了模具拔模角需盡可能小。須保持與配合尺寸相關的重點尺寸。
	✔ 倍斯特與ABC相互理解保持產品編號A5197有限公差範圍的尺寸比其它產品困難，即使倍斯特已使用最高的材料來降低模具耗損。
週會	✔ 每週電話會議將在每星期五早上六點（洛杉磯時間）／晚上十點（臺灣時間）舉行，以更新新產品開發的進度。
其它議題	✔ ABC訪問倍斯特工廠是否成行，取決於產品發展進度。

關鍵字彙

meeting minutes *(ph.)* [ˈmiːtiŋ 'minits] **會議記錄**

同義詞 cahier, meeting notes

相關詞 in a minute 立刻；to the minute 準時；minute book 記錄簿

without objection *(ph.)* **無異議**

同義詞 no contest, no dissenting voices, unanimity

反義詞 raise an objection, call in question, file objection 提出異議

come off *(ph.)* [kʌm`ɔf] **實現、發生**

同義詞 happen, occur, take place

相關詞 Come off it! 別吹牛了；come off second-best 位居第二；come off one's high horse 不再驕傲自大

關鍵句型

as shown on the next page 如下頁所示

例句說明

Please refer to the shipping requirement breaking down **as shown on the next page**.

➡ 請參閱裝船需求分列如下頁所示。

The piece price was adjusted **as shown on the next page**.

➡ 產品單價調整如下頁所示。

替換句型

The piece price was adjusted as particularized overleaf.

勵志小格言

It's fine to celebrate success, but it is more important to heed the lessons of failure.

～Bill Gates, Microsoft Co-founder

慶祝勝利是好的，但吸取失敗的教訓更重要。 *～微軟創辦者　比爾蓋茲*

知識補給

在與客戶會議之前先依據與會雙方欲討論的議題彙整出一份會議議程（meeting agenda），站在以客為尊的立場，通常是由出口端，及我方提供會議議程，但即使已事先擬定主題，會議中不見得會依據議程逐一討論，也可能出現臨時動議。因此，會議紀錄者即扮演著舉足輕重的角色，而會議記錄者通常也由我方擔任，除了要能精通雙方語言，同時須對主題十分了解，在各項議題穿插討論過程中，能記錄細節且抓住要點，以依據雙方討論結果提供完整且正確之會議紀錄（meeting minutes）。

職場經驗談

會議中你來我往的討論，對於雙方提出的建議及想法，會議紀錄者盡可能詳盡地記下每一個細節，做為會後檢視及回顧的依據。但將討論結果彙整成會議紀錄時，則須著重在討論要點及最終結論。會議記錄如同重點筆記，應簡潔卻切入要點。

不論身為深淺或資深的國貿從業人員，在與國外客戶開會時可隨時錄音存檔討論過程，做為日後參考，尤其是在雙方對結論出現分歧時之依據。

菜鳥變達人

中翻英練習

1. 基姆很高興有這個機會參加貿易展。

2. 到展覽館的路線圖如下頁所示。

中翻英解答

1 Kim was pleased to have this opportunity of attending the trade show.

2 The route map to the exhibition hall is indicated as shown on the next page.

1-3-5 送樣審核
PPAP Verification

★情境說明

ABC Co. advises Best Corp. of the details of PPAP Verification.
ABC公司通知倍斯特公司送樣審核細節。

★角色介紹

（買方）Buyer: ABC Co., Ltd.
（賣方）Seller: Best International Trade Corp.

情境對話

B: Hi, Olivia. This is Wesley Yang from Best Corp. I'm calling to speak about the sample preparation for part number A5197.

B: 您好，奧利維亞。我是倍斯特公司的衛斯理，我打電話是要談產品編號A5197樣品製備的事。

A: Did everything go smoothly?

A: 一切進行得順利嗎？

B: Kind of. Ten pieces of cosmetic samples are ready for delivery to ISH hall for your exhibition purpose.

B: 算是。十件外觀樣品已準備送到ISH展館，供貴司展覽用。

A: Appreciate.

A: 感謝。

B: The bad news is the critical dimension 2.50 +0.05/-0.25 being still slightly out of upper limit to 2.552, after several times of tooling adjustment. I was wondering could it be possible to modify the matting part to match 2.552. Or else, may we request some pieces of matting parts for assembly reference?

B: 壞消息是在調整模具數次後，重點尺寸2.50±0.05/-0.25仍略超出上限至2.552。我想是否可能修改配件來配合2.552，亦或我們可以要求一些配件做為組配基準？

A: I must talk with our engineering team about this.

A: 我必須與我們的工程團隊談談。

B: Sure. When will we be getting the feedback?

B: 當然。最早什麼時候會有回音？

A: I'll try to work it out and give you a specific direction in this week.

A: 我會試著在本週有個結果，並給您一個明確的指示。

關鍵字彙

speak about *(ph.)* [spi:kəˈbaut] **提到、談論**

同義詞 talk about, speak of, refer

相關詞 speak out, speak up 大聲說；to speak of 值得一提的

kind of *(ph.)* [kaind ɔv] **有一點**

同義詞 sort of, somewhat, kinda

相關詞 sth. of the kind 諸如此類的事物；nothing of the kind 一點都不像；one-of-a-kind 獨一無二的

out of *(ph.)* [aut ɔv] **在…範圍外**

同義詞 outside of, beyond；exceed

相關詞 out of range 超出範圍；out of season 過了旺季；out of sight 超出視線

upper limit *(ph.)* [ˈʌpə ˈlɪmɪt] **上限**

同義詞 maximum, superior limit, upper bound

相關詞 upper limit value 上限值；upper limits of normal 正常上限

match *(v.)* [mætʃ] **和…相配**

同義詞 fit, mate

相關詞 match up 使相配；match up to 比得過；match with 相配

specific direction *(ph.)* [spəˈsɪfɪk dəˈrekʃn] **具體方向**

同義詞 concrete direction, definite direction, previse instruction

相關詞 specific performance 具體履行；specific meaning 特定含意；be more specific 更具體

關鍵句型

A very much regret to announce B⋯　A十分抱歉通知B⋯

例句說明

I very much regret to announce you that we are unable to accept your kind invitation of the end-year party.

➡ 我十分抱歉通知您我司不克接受貴司年終尾牙派對的盛情邀約。

My boss very much regretted to announce our team of layoffs notice.

➡ 老闆十分遺憾地通知組員有關裁員的通知。

替換句型

It is with the greatest regret that my boss informed our team of layoffs notice.

In response to mail/calling of date　回覆某日來函／來電

例句說明

In response to your mail of yesterday, please arrange the air shipment with fright prepaid.

➡ 茲回覆您昨日來函，請安排貴司付費空運。

In response to Erica's mail of March 23, we can only accept the air shipment with freight collection.

➡ 茲回覆艾瑞卡三月二十三日來函，我司僅能接受運費到付空運。

替換句型

Answering Erica's mail of March 23, we can only accept the air shipment with freight collection.

勵志小格言

Sensitive people suffer more, but they love more and dream more.

敏感的人承受更多，但他們有更多的愛和更多的夢想。

～摘錄至網 www.livelifehappy.com

英文書信這樣寫

Dear Wesley,

In response to your requirement by yesterday's call, I very much regret to announce you that our engineering team can't accept the critical dimension adjusted to 2.552 for part number A5197 due to assembly concern. Please kick off tooling modification to correct the dimension more precisely. In the meanwhile, five pieces of matting parts were sent to your Taichung plant in accordance with your requirement. Please confirm upon the receipt of them.

Sent with this, you may see the required sample quantity of initial PPAP and formal PPAP respectively to be submitted along with PPAP documentation. We are deeply convinced the benefit of phased PPAP is highlighting the actual status of production run, and do appreciate you work closely with other engineering team to drive PPAP approval.

Shall there be anything we could do for you, please never hesitate to head up.

Yours sincerely,
Olivia Porter

中文翻譯

衛斯理您好：

特此回答貴司昨日來電所提出之要求，我很遺憾通知您，由於裝配考量，我司工程團隊無法接受產品編號A5197的重點尺寸調整為2.552。請啟動模具修改使尺寸更精確。與此同時，五件配合件已按照您的要求發送到貴司台中廠，請確認查收。

如您所視，隨函覆上須與PPAP檔一同提交的初始PPAP和正式PPAP分別所需的樣品數量。我司深信，階段性PPAP的好處是突顯生產運作的實際狀況，並感激貴司與我司工程團隊密切配合促成PPAP核可。

有任何需要效勞的地方，請不吝提出。

奧莉維亞波特　敬啟

知識補給

PPAP（Production Part Approval Process）生產件批准程式:

PPAP的目的是用來確定供應商是否已經正確理解了顧客工程設計和規範的要求，以及供應商生產過程是否具有潛在能力生產該產品，並在實際生產過程中按所規定的生產步驟來滿足顧客要求的產品質量。

以上資料來源參考智庫百科網頁http://www.mbalib.com

職場經驗談

簡而言之，所謂PPAP（Production Part Approval Process）生產件批准程式，就是產品在正式量產前，供應商或製造商為了證明自家的生產製程有能力生產該產品，且生產的產品能符合客戶不論是製程、尺寸、外觀、功能等等規範及要求，而將打樣樣品遞交給客戶端審核之流程。送樣審核之要求依各客戶定義之，但一般來說送樣核可後（PPAP Approval），客戶會發予核可證書（PSW, Part Submission Warrant），作為供應商或製造商後續啟動大量生產的依據；反之，則送樣判退（PPAP Rejection），須依據客戶要求重新送樣（Re-PPAP Submission）。

菜鳥變達人

中翻英練習

1. 我很遺憾地通知新人未通過試用。

2. 茲回覆面試者本週一來函，面試者已獲得錄取。

中翻英解答

1 I very much regret to announce the new employee is unqualified.

2 In response to the interviewee's mail of this Monday, the interviewee got the position.

2-1 參加商展
Participation in Trade Exhibition

2-2 商務旅行
Business Travel

2-3 客戶來訪
Visitation

商務活動
Commercial Activities

Part2

2-1 參加商展
Participation in Trade Exhibition

2-1-1 報名參展
Application for Trade Exhibition

★情境說明

Best Corp. calls the organizer of the trade show to inquire application issue.

倍斯特公司致電展覽單位詢問報名參展事宜。

★角色介紹

（貿易展主辦單位）Organizer of trade show: Messe Frankfurt

（展商）Vendor: Best International Trade Corp.

情境對話

B: Hi, we would like to participate in next ISH show. When will you start accepting registration?

B: 您好！我們想參加下屆ISH展。何時開始接受報名？

O: The application is open now. Is this your first time participating in ISH show?

O: 報名已經開始。這是貴司首次參展嗎？

B: Yes, it is.

B: 是的。

O: Please download the application form, and return it after fill in. You must pay a deposit in advance and send us the receipt along with the form.

O: 請直接下載報名表，完成填表後寄回。您必續先預付訂金，並將匯款收據連同報名表寄回。

B: What is the deadline for the application?

B: 何時截止報名？

O: Registration ends on the last day of this month. To ensure you fill in the form correctly, you must read the instruction firstly.

O: 本月底是截止日。為確保您能正確填寫此表, 請仔細閱讀填表須知。

B: When can we have the booth number?

B: 何時可知道攤位號碼？

O: The organizer will allocate the booth after conducting vendor qualification and send formal notification accordingly.

O: 主辦單位完成展商審核後會進行攤位分配，並寄發正式通知。

B: I see. Thank you.

B: 我瞭解了。謝謝您！

關鍵字彙

participate in *(ph.)* 參加

同義詞 take part in, join in, partake in

相關詞 participate in the discussion 參加討論；participate in new product development 參與新產品開發

registration *(n.)* [ˌrɛdʒɪ`streʃən] 登記

同義詞 enrollment

相關詞 registration form 登記表；Business Registration Certificate 商業登記證

application form *(ph.)* 申請表、報名表

同義詞 registration form, entry form, enrolment form

相關詞 application form in quadruplicate 申請表一式四份；on-line application form 線上報名表

deadline *(n.)* [`dɛdˌlaɪn] 截止日期、最後期限

同義詞 expiration date, due date

相關詞 submission deadline 提交期限

allocate *(v.)* [`æləˌket] 分配

同義詞 assign, allot, portion

相關詞 allocate cargo 配貨

qualification *(n.)* [ˌkwɑləfə`keʃən] 資格

同義詞 eligibility, fitness

相關詞 qualification rate of product 產品合格率

關鍵句型

When is the deadline? 截止日為何?

例句說明

Please remark **when the deadline** for sample submission is.

➡ 請備註送樣截止為何。

Please advise **when the deadline** of the loading period is.

➡ 請告知裝運截止日為何。

替換句型

Please remark what the allotted time for sample submission is.

Please advise what the time limit of the loading period is.

To ensure sth. , sb. must… 為確保某事，某人需…

例句說明

To ensure product quality and cheap, **the manufacturer must** be careful with cost containment and quality control.

➡ 為確保物美價廉，製造商需審慎成本控制及品質管控。

To ensure the product meet specification and standard, **QA department must** implement performance test.

➡ 為確保產品符合規範及標準，品保部門需進行功能性測試。

替換句型

To make certain that the quality and cheap, cost containment, and quality control are necessary for the manufacturer.

勵志小格言

Do not, for one repulse, give up the purpose that you resolved to effect.

～*William Shakespeare, English playwright*

不要只因一次失敗，就放棄你原來決心想達到的目的。 ～*英國劇作家　莎士比亞*

知識補給

參展報名流程：線上登錄→繳納訂金→郵寄報名→資格審核→攤位規劃→確認參展資格（不合格→退回訂金／合格→開立訂金收據）→展前說明會（決定攤位位置）→繳交費用→會展相關作業申請→進場裝潢→開展

相關的報名程序仍依各主辦單位而異，大致上而言概要如下:

- 報名時間：國際性展覽約在展期前的10～12個月開始報名。
- 報名方式：參加過展覽的展商，主辦單位會主動寄發報名表。首次參展的展商可在主辦單位網站下載報名表。需詳細閱讀報名表後的相關規定，將填妥後之報名表及繳納訂金的匯款單一同郵寄給主辦單位，由主辦單位進行展商資格審核及攤位規劃。
- 攤位規劃：展商對主辦單位分配的攤位位置有異議時，可提出申請更換，但好的展位通常是一位難求，所以原則上仍依主辦單位安排為主。
- 進場裝潢：展位的設計一般會委由專業設計公司依據展商所分配到的展位位置、展品形式及展商預算等進行規劃。尤其是在海外參展或首次參展的展商，建議由有經驗的專業設計公司承攬設計、派工、監工到驗收，一手包辦。當然較具規模的大型企業，一般會由自己公司所屬的展位設計團隊負責。但需特別注意的是，需在主辦單位規定的時間內進場裝潢及如期完工。

報名表範本：

以下表格擷取自Mega Show 網站http://www.mega-show.com/

STAND SPACE APPLICATION FORM 攤位申請表格

Asian 亞洲禮品及贈品展
GIFTS & PREMIUMS SHOW MEGA SHOW Series
20 - 23 October 2014
HONG KONG CONVENTION & EXHIBITION CENTRE
香港會議展覽中心

MEGA SHOW PART 1
20 - 23 October 2014

PART ONE 第一部份

COMPANY INFORMATION 公司資料

Please fill in this form carefully as the information provided will be used for listing in the fair catalogue. (Please fill out in block letters)
請小心填寫此表格，貴公司所提供之資料將刊登於展覽會場刊內。(請以英文正楷填寫)

Name of Company 公司名稱：

Address 地址：

Postal Code 郵編： Country 國家：

Tel No. 電話： Fax No. 傳真：

E-mail 電子郵件：

Web Site 網址：

Person to contact concerning your participation in the fair 有關參展事務之聯絡人

Name 姓名 (Mr. / Ms.)：

Position 職位：

Product Brand Name (s) 產品牌子名稱：

EXHIBITS 展品項目

*Please tick appropriate box(es) and specify products 請選擇類別及列明有關產品

☐ Gifts 禮 品：

☐ Premiums 贈 品：

☐ Others 其 他：

C1186042-MSAF-GIFTS-AF-AM

MEGA EXPO | Trade Media Partner: AASource.com | Supporting Organisation: mehk | Join us on: facebook | TRADE BUYERS ONLY | www.mega-show.com

職場經驗談

每年世界各地各行各業皆會舉辦大大小小展覽，選擇符合自身企業屬性的展覽要先考量該展覽是否涵蓋了您的銷售市場，並非大城市舉辦的大型展覽就是適合的地點，展覽地須能吸引潛在客戶群，而且必須是符合產品導向，例如能符合產品生產排程、展期可配合新產品上市時間，且能符合相應的產品廣告等，畢竟參展費用可是一筆可觀的數目。

菜鳥變達人

中翻英練習

1. 為了確保準時交貨，你必須隨時注意生產進度。

---

2. 人事公告公布的截止日是何時？

中翻英解答

1 To ensure punctual shipment, you must always pay attention to the production progress.

2 What's the deadline to publish the personnel announcement?

2-1-2 邀請觀展
Invitation to the Trade Exhibition

★情境說明

Best Corp. invites existing customers to visit the exhibition.

倍斯特公司邀請既有客戶參觀展覽。

★角色介紹

（買方）Buyer: ABC Co., Ltd.

（賣方）Seller: Best International Trade Corp.

情境對話

B: Hi. I'm calling for Olivia Porter.	B: 您好！我找奧莉維亞 波特。
A: Olivia speaking.	A: 我是奧莉維亞。
B: This is Wesley Yang at Best. Corp. I'm calling to invite you to visit our booth at the ISH Show.	B: 我是倍斯特公司的衛斯理 楊。我致電是要邀請您參觀我們在ISH展的攤位。
A: Thanks for your invitation.	A: 感謝您的邀請。

B: Our latest brochure will be available then, and we will release our new product in the show.

B: 屆時將會有最新的產品目錄，並且我們會在展覽會發表新品。

A: Sounds great. I'll be sure to drop by. How can I find you booth?

A: 聽起來好極了。我一定會過去參觀。如何找到貴司的攤位？

B: Our booth number is 1E/23 located at the corner in section A. I'll e-mail you an invitation letter.

B: 我們的攤位號碼是1E／23，位在A區的拐角處。我會將邀請函電郵給您。

A: Thank you. I'm looking forward to seeing you at the show.

A: 感謝您。期待在展覽會與您碰面。

關鍵字彙

visit *(v.)* [`vɪzɪt] **參觀**

同義詞 drop in, call on, attend

相關詞 visiting card 名片；return visit 重訪、再次光顧

booth *(n.)* [buθ] **攤位**

同義詞 stall, stand

相關詞 booth bunny 商展中的促銷女郎

show *(n.)* [ʃo] **展覽**

同義詞 exhibition, fair, expo

相關詞 on show 被展覽；show room 展示廳

available *(a.)* [ə`veləb!] **可用的、可得的**

同義詞 obtainable, ready

相關詞 projected available balance 預計可用庫存

drop by *(ph.)* **順道拜訪**

同義詞 drop over, stop in, come over

解析 商業行為中常用於指拜訪對方展覽攤位、公司、工廠

look forward to *(ph.)* **期待**

同義詞 expect, anticipate, hope

解析 商業書信中常用於結尾表示期待對方回覆訊息

關鍵句型

be sure to 務必

例句說明

Be sure to keep in touch with me.

➡ 務必與我保持聯繫。

I'll be sure to reply within two weeks after receive your notice.

➡ 我在接到通知後的兩週內必定回信。

替換句型

Keep in touch with me by all means.

勵志小格言

Failure is the condiment that gives success its flavor.

~ Truman Capote, Writer

失敗是使成功變美味的調味料。

~ 作家　楚門　卡波提

英文書信這樣寫

Issued Invitation Letter to Existing Customers with Individual Name

Dear Olivia,

It's my great pleasure, on behalf of Best International Trade Corp., to invite you to visit our booth at ISH show from March 24th to 29th, 2015.

Our business team and I will be there to handle the booth during the exhibition time, and I would be glad to show you our latest product. You may refer to the exhibition information as below, and please drop by any time.

Booth No.: 1E/23 and 1E/25

Date: March 24th ~ March 29th, 2015

Venue: Messe Frankfurt (Ludwig-Erhard-Anlage 1 60327 Frankfurt, Hesse, Germany)

If you would like to make an appointment during the exhibit hours, please drop me a message. I can then ensure your meeting time is reserved.

Do come and join us. We anticipate to see you at the ISH Show.

Sincerely yours,
Wesley Yang

中文翻譯

（以個人名義發送邀請函予既有客戶）

奧莉維亞您好：

在此謹代表倍斯特公司非常榮幸的邀請您參觀我司在ISH展的攤位，展期為2015年3月24日至29日。

我司的業務團隊及本人將會在展覽期間處理攤位事宜，我將非常樂意為您展示我司最新的產品。請參閱下列展覽相關訊息，隨時歡迎您光臨。

攤位號碼：1E／23
展覽期間：2015年3月24日至29日。
展覽地點：Messe Frankfurt（Ludwig-Erhard-Anlage 1 60327 Frankfurt, Hesse, Germany）

如您欲在展覽期間進行會談，請與我聯絡，以確保為您事先保留會議時間。

歡迎您出席。我們十分期待在ISH展與您見面。

衛斯理　楊　敬啟

知識補給

邀請觀展的對象大致來說可分為兩大類：既有客戶群及潛在客戶群

既有客戶群：即與我方已有交易往來之客戶，以信函或電郵的方式寄發邀請函，邀請函需署名特定對象，以表邀請誠意及避免信函郵件被視垃圾郵件或廣告信函而被忽略。

潛在客戶群：簡而言之就是未曾交易往來之客戶，由於無法掌握確切特定對象，可藉由傳播工具宣傳公司，吸引客戶觀展時駐足我方攤位，例如善用公司網頁宣傳及參展展商名錄，或另付費在產業期刊或主辦單位的網站或文宣中做宣傳。

職場經驗談

對於公司舉足輕重的重要客戶，可在寄發邀請函前親自致電邀約，除了可表達我方邀請觀展之誠意外，也可詢問對方預計觀展之人員及人數，在寄發邀請函時附上展覽入場券。另可先預約會議時間，我方可在展覽會場事先安排展位位置或規劃的小型會議間進行會晤討論。

菜鳥變達人

中翻英練習

1. 請務必準時出貨。

2. 線上報名的截止日為何？

中翻英解答

1 Be sure to make punctual shipment.

2 When is the deadline of the on-line application?

2-1-3 會展接待
Serving the Visitors

★情境說明

Best Corp. serves visitors dropping by their booth.

倍斯特公司在會展招呼參觀其展位的訪客。

★角色介紹

（訪客）Visitor

（賣方）Seller: Best International Trade Corp.

情境對話

B: Good morning, Sir. Is anything you'd like to take an interest in?

B: 早安，先生。有任何東西您感興趣嗎？

V: Just looking around.

V: 只是隨便看看。

B: Here is our product list for your reference.

B: 這是我們的產品目錄，供您參考。

V: Thank you.

V: 感謝您。

B: May I have your contact information?

B: 我可以索取您的聯繫資料嗎？

V: Sure. This is my business card.	V: 當然。這是我的名片。
B: Nice to meet you, Mr. Mitsui. Here is mine. Please call me anytime if you need further information. You can always reach me on my mobile phone.	B: 很高興見到您，三井先生。這是我的名片。如果需要進一步訊息，請隨時與我聯繫。您隨時打我的手機都能找到我。
V: I will, Mr. Yang. BTW, I want to attend the seminar on the internet marketing. Do you know where is the exhibition hall ?	V: 我會的，楊先生。對了，我想參加網路行銷研討會。您知道展覽廳在哪嗎？
B: The seminar is in Hall # 6 on the third floor.	B：這次研討會是在三樓的六號廳舉行。
V: Got it. Thank you.	V：知道了。謝謝您！
B: Don't mention it. Have a good time at the seminar, Mr. Mitsui.	B: 別客氣。祝您在研討會上愉快，三井先生。

關鍵字彙

interest *(n.)* [`ɪntərɪst] **興趣、愛好**

同義詞 concern

相關詞 interest payment 利息支付；interest rate 利率

look around *(ph.)* **環顧四週**

同義詞 look about saunter up and down

解析 指沒有特別目的四處看，展覽中常會有非產業的訪客，並無目的尋找特別產品，單純只是閒逛。如有特殊目的尋找則常用字彙有look for, search for。

reference *(n.)* [`rɛfərəns] **參考、參照**

同義詞 consultation

相關詞 cross-reference 互相參造

contact *(n.)* [`kantækt] **聯繫**

同義詞 connect

相關詞 contact information, contact details 聯繫資料

business card *(ph.)* **名片**

同義詞 visiting card, calling card

解析 商業行為中首次見面時交換名片為基本禮儀，藉以取得對方聯繫資料，及了解對方職稱。

reach *(v.)* [ritʃ] **取得聯繫、達成**

同義詞 contact, get in touch；come to

相關詞 reach an agreement 達成協議

關鍵句型

take an interest in sth. 想瞭解某事

例句說明

Our product are well-known to the buyers who **take an interest in** the industrial market.

➡ 我司的產品在熱衷於工業市場的買家中是眾所皆知的。

My customer **takes a great interest in** the new material of your product.

➡ 我的顧客對於貴司產品的新材質十分感興趣。

替換句型

The client wants to learn something about the new material of your product.

for one's reference 提供予某人參考

例句說明

We are sending a catalogue **for your reference**.

➡ 我們寄了一本目錄供你方參考.

We shall appreciate it, if you will provide new pattern **for our reference**.

➡ 如能提供我們新花色作為參考，我司將不甚感激。

替換句型

For more specific product information, please refer to our website.

英文書信這樣寫

Dear Mr. Mitsui,

"O ha yo u go za i ma su !" Please accept our thanks for your visitation to our booth during the ISH show.

I'd like to know if you have had the chance to look at the catalogue offered you at the show yet. Just to be sure, enclosed please find another catalogue.

We're pleased to have this opportunity of reminding you that the exclusive discount of exhibition will expire at the end of month. You're suggested to grasp this chance to place an initial order by the deadline.

We hope that we may be of service to you and believe you will be satisfied with our products.

Yours sincerely,
Wesley Yang

中文翻譯

三井先生您好：

「上午好！」感謝您於ISH展時造訪我司展位。

我想知道您是否有機會看了會展時提供給您的目錄。為了以防萬一，隨函附上另一份目錄。

我們很高興有這個機會提醒您，展覽的獨家折扣將在本月底到期。建議你抓住這個機會在截止日前下首張訂單。

希望我司可以為您服務，相信您會滿意我司的產品。

衛斯理　楊　敬啟

勵志小格言

Courage is resistance to fear, mastery of fear – not absence of fear.

~ Mark Twain, Writer

勇氣是抗拒恐懼，征服恐懼 – 不是沒有恐懼。　*～作家　馬克　吐溫*

知識補給

參加國外展覽是行銷計畫的一環，由於展覽的準備期很長，在決定參加某一展覽之後，最好成立工作小組或指定專人負責規劃。工作小組除負責與主辦單位連絡外，亦同時負責推動部分參展工作、控制進度及各單位間之協調配合。展前準備工作必須配合主辦單位之進度，依照展覽舉辦頻率的不同，最早可能在展出前一年多就必須開始，比較晚者，至少亦須於展前半年推動。

詳細資訊可參閱《「廠商赴國外參展標準流程（SOP）及應注意事項：中華民國對外貿易發展協會98.11.25編撰」》。

職場經驗談

展期通常不超過一週，如何在短時間達到最高經濟效益，是參展的最主要目的，因此參展人員扮演舉足輕重的腳色，進行展前的培訓及準備工作相當重要，尤其針對首次參與展覽的新生菜鳥。培訓須著重在對產品的熟悉度，如產品規格、型號、顏色等。要能現場實際操作產品，也須清楚產品性能及如何操作，並要瞭解各展品在攤位中的相關擺設位置。

參展人員需在展館中與陌生人交談、介紹產品、發送印刷品或精品，因此身為參展人的您若能具備樂於跟陌生人交談的個性，必能更駕輕就熟。

菜鳥變達人

中翻英練習

1. 貴司的業務代表多久出訪客戶一次？

2. 我想瞭解貴司的組織架構。

中翻英解答

1 How often does your sales representative visit customers?

2 I take an interest in the organization chart of your company.

2-1-4 展品介紹
Introduction of Exhibits

★情境說明

Best Corp. introduces the product to potential customer.
倍斯特公司對潛在客戶介紹產品。

★角色介紹

（潛在客戶）Potential Customer
（賣方）Seller: Best International Trade Corp.

情境對話

B: Hi. May I show you our best-selling products?	B: 您好！我可以拿我們的暢銷品讓您看看嗎？
P: I'm looking for 3/4" ball valve.	P: 我在尋找 3／4英吋的球閥。
B: I'm sorry. We don't showcase this size this time, but you can find it on our product list. Please take a look.	B: 抱歉，我們這次展覽並未陳列該尺寸，但您可以在我們的產品目錄中找到它。請查閱。
P: Is it regular brass or low-lead brass?	P: 這是一般銅或低鉛銅？

B: We have both materials.

B: 兩種材質都有。

P: Can it comply with MSS-SP-110 standard?

P: 是否可符合MSS-SP-110 規範？

B: Definitely. The validation test report will be normally attached along with each shipment for customer's examination.

B: 這是絕對地。通常每批出貨都會附上合格檢驗報告，供客戶檢視。

P: May I have a sample for review?

P: 我可否要一個樣品進行檢視？

B: Sure. The sample will be sent out once I return to the office. I'm sure you will be very pleased with the high quality of our product.

B: 當然。待我回辦公室後會寄出樣品。我確信您會非常滿意我司產品的高質量。

P: I'm also interested in your circulator valve.

P：我對你們的蒸汽球閥也很感興趣。

B: Here are 1/2" circulator valve and 3/4" circulator valve coming in two different types, T x TMU and CUP x TMU respectively.

B：這裡是1／2英吋蒸氣球閥和3／4英吋蒸氣球閥，有兩種不同的類型，分別是把手牙口式及把手焊接式。

關鍵字彙

look for *(ph.)* **尋找**

同義詞 seek, search

解析 嘗試找出或發現某物，但尚未找到。不同於“find”，指已找到。

showcase *(v.)* [ˋʃoˌkes] **陳列**

同義詞 put on display

相關詞 showcase export zone 出口展覽區

material *(n.)* [məˋtɪrɪəl] **材質**

同義詞 composition, substance

相關詞 raw material 原料；bill of material (BOM) 材料清單

comply with *(ph.)* **遵從、符合**

同義詞 be eligible for, be corresponding to, conform to

相關詞 comply with government safety regulations 符合政府安全規定

examination *(n.)* [ɪgˌzæməˋneʃən] **檢查、調查**

同義詞 inspection, investigation, audit, analysis

相關詞 finished product examination 成品檢驗

customer *(n.)* [ˋkʌstəmɚ] **顧客、買主**

同義詞 consumer, client, purchaser, buyer, vendee

相關詞 customer value 客戶價值；customer-driven 顧客導向

關鍵句型

I'm sure… 我確信…

例句說明

I'm sure we could reach an agreement.

➡ 我確認我們會達成共識。

I'm 100 percent sure to pay by T/T today.

➡ 我百分之百確定今天會電匯付款。

替換句型

I make certain of transferring the payment today.

Sb. be pleased with 某人對…感到滿意

例句說明

I'm very pleased with the quality of your product.

➡ 我很滿意貴司的產品品質。

The customer was not pleased with the production progress we are making.

➡ 客戶對於我們的生產進度不甚滿意。

替換句型

The customer was not gratified the production progress we are making.

英文書信這樣寫

Dear Joan,

It's a pleasure to meet you at the ISH show last month.

This email serves (as a reminder) to inform you that the sample of 3/4" ball valve you required was sent out today. We also enclosed two samples each of 1/2" circulator valve and 3/4"circulator valve with below specification by the same air parcel post. Your confirmation in receipt of the samples by return will be highly appreciated.

● CIRCULATOR VALVE - T x TMU	● CIRCULATOR VALVE - CUP x TMU
● UB-425	● UB-426
● Forged brass body	● Forged brass body
● 1/4 Turn design	● 1/4 Turn design
● Straight pattern	● Straight pattern
● FIP x Male union	● Solder x Male union
● Phenolic resin heat resistant handle	● Phenolic resin heat resistant handle
● 150WSP-600WOG	● 150WSP-600WOG
● Size:1/2" & 3/4"	● Size:1/2" & 3/4"

We're waiting for your response in this matter and always ready to service you anytime.

Yours sincerely,
Wesley Yang

中文翻譯

瓊您好：

很榮幸在上個月的ISH展見到您。

這封電郵是通知您，您所需的3／4” 球閥樣品已於今日寄出。我們還附上了兩件樣品在相同的航空包裹中，分別是以下所列規格的1 ／ 2” 蒸氣球閥和3／4” 蒸氣球閥。您能回函確認收到樣品，我司不勝感激。

● 蒸氣球閥 - 把手牙口式	● 蒸氣球閥 - 把手焊接式
● Forged brass body	● Forged brass body
● 1/4 Turn design	● 1/4 Turn design
● Straight pattern	● Straight pattern
● FIP x Male union	● Solder x Male union
● Phenolic resin heat resistant handle	● Phenolic resin heat resistant handle
● 150WSP-600WOG	● 150WSP-600WOG
● Size:1/2" & 3/4"	● Size:1/2" & 3/4"

我司等待您對此事的回覆，並隨時準備為您服務。

衛斯理　楊　敬啟

勵志小格言

KEEPING GOING. Everything you need will come to you at the perfect time.

~ from website lessonslearnedinlife.com

保持前進。你需要的一切會在完美的時間來找你。

～摘錄自網站 lessonslearnedinlife.com

知識補給

展期一般為五天，展館開放時間為每日八個小時，所謂「時間就是金錢」，在展館中的每一分每一秒都是極為珍貴，如何把握有限的時間達到最高的效益，能分辨並把握住目標客戶即是關鍵。但展館為公共開放空間，觀展者不一定都是買家，所以針對駐足展位的觀展者須在最快的時間內寒暄交談並確認對方身分，確認對方為目標客戶群後則可進行名片交換，然後紀錄下對方所尋找的目標產品，作為展後追蹤跟進的依據。

職場經驗談

如前文所提，展覽時間有限，不只展商需把握分分秒秒，觀展者也會儘可能在有限的時間內駐足更多的展位，所以可以掌握「快、很、準」 的原則。「快」速確認身分，「很」快進入主題，及「準」確紀錄資料，尤其是對方主要尋找商品或我方在會展中口頭提供的訊息都需重點紀錄，但不建議在會展中對首次交談客戶進行書面或口頭報價。

菜鳥變達人

中翻英練習

1. 陳先生對你的回答感到滿意。

2. 我確信這只不過是一次以計算失誤。

中翻英解答

1 Mr. Chen was pleased with your response.

2 I'm sure it is just some sort of error in calculation.

2-1-5 展後拜訪
Visitation Plan to Potential Customer Meeting in the Exhibition

★情境說明

Best Corp. plans to visit potential customer meeting in the exhibition.

倍斯特公司於展後計畫拜訪參觀展位的潛在客戶。

★角色介紹

（潛在客戶）Potential Customer

（賣方）Seller: Best International Trade Corp.

情境對話

B: Hello! Mr. Douglas, this is Wesley Yang calling from Best Corp. We've met at our booth during the ISH show last month.

B: 您好！道格拉斯先生。我是倍斯特公司的衛斯理 楊。我們上個月在我司的ISH展攤位見過面。

P: Yes, I remember you, Mr. Yang.

P: 是的，我記得您，楊先生。

B: Really appreciate your visiting to our booth. I recalled that you inquired about our 3/4" ball valve and have

B: 非常感激您參觀我們的展位。我記得的您詢問我們的3／4英吋球閥，

already sent samples to you per your request.

我們並且已依據您的需求寄出樣品。

P: I already got the samples. Thank you.

P: 我已經收到樣品了。謝謝您！

B: We'd like to hear your input about our product. I wonder if it is convenient for me to visit you in week 16.

B: 我們想聽聽您對於我司產品的看法。不知是否方便我在第十六週參訪貴司。

P: I'll fly to England on business on the first two days of that week. You can come over after I get back.

P: 第十六週的前兩天我將出差英國。您可以在我回來後來訪。

B: How about April 17?

B: 4月17日如何？

P: OK. That will be fine.

P: 好的，這個時間很好。

B: Good. I will email my itinerary for your reference.

B: 太好了。我會將我的行程電郵給您參考。

關鍵字彙

recall *(v.)* [rɪ`kɔl] **回想**

同義詞 remember, recollect, reminisce

相關詞 product recall 產品召回

input *(n.)* [`ɪn͵pʊt] **（資金、材料、勞動力等）投入、投資**

同義詞 comment, remark

解析 商業中常用來指對方提供的反饋、建議等。例如: His report provides us with useful input of corrective actions. 他報告內容的改善對策為我們提供有效見解。

convenient *(a.)* [kən`vinjənt] **方便的、合宜的**

同義詞 favorable, suitable

相關詞 convenient time 合宜的時間

week 16 *(ph.)* **第十六週**

解析 商業行為中，歐洲國家習慣以週數來表達時間區間，如預計出差期間、預計到貨期間等。而2014年第16週，則指2014年4月13日至4月19日。

get back *(ph.)* **返回、回來**

同義詞 come back, return

相關詞 get back on one's feet 恢復正常

itinerary *(n.)* [aɪ`tɪnə͵rɛrɪ] **旅程計畫**

同義詞 travel plan

相關詞 itinerary arrangement 行程安排

關鍵句型

be convenient to (for) sb. 對某人是方便的

例句說明

Call me at any time when it **is convenient to** you.

➡ 任何您方便的時候就來電。

It **is not convenient for** me to ring her up.

➡ 我現在不便於致電給她。

替換句型

We will call her at the proper time

It is not the proper time for me to ring her up.

fly to some place on business 到某地出差

例句說明

Did you **fly to New York on business** or for pleasure last month?

➡ 你上個月到紐約是洽公還是遊玩？

Annie **flied to Tokyo on business**.

➡ 安妮到東京出差。

替換句型

Annie went on a business trip to Tokyo.

Annie went to Tokyo on business.

Annie was sent to Tokyo on a business trip.

Annie was away on a business trip to Tokyo.

勵志小格言

There are no secrets to success. It is the result of preparation, hard work, and learning from failure.

~ Colin Powell, U.S. Secretary of State

成功沒有祕訣，它是準備、勤奮及由失敗學習的結果。 *～美國國務卿　克林　鮑威爾*

英文書信這樣寫

Dear Mr. Douglas,

We were pleased to see you during the ISH show last month and it's a pleasure to learn you're interested in our 3/4" ball valve.

I'm going to be on a business trip to your city in week 16 and wondering if you will be available to meet me to talk about further cooperation plan.

Please let me know if the arrangement is convenient for you. If not, please advise when the most convenient time for my visit is.

Looking forward to your early reply.

Yours sincerely,
Wesley Yang

中文翻譯

道格拉斯先生您好，

我們很高興上個月能在ISH展見到您，以及知道貴司對我們的3／4英吋球閥感興趣。

我將在第十六週造訪貴司所在城市，屆時不知您是否方便與我會面談談未來合作計畫。

請讓我知道這項安排對您來說是否方便。若否，請告知何時拜訪您最方便。

期待你的早日答覆。

衛斯理　楊　敬啟

知識補給

展前期：展商通常會在開展前二至三天抵達會場作展前準備，如裝潢點交，確認裝潢設計符合所需要求，如有些微差異處可及時進行修改。工班依據設計圖進行施工，很少情況下會有極大誤差，即使如此，展期將至，也不建議大興土木進行修改。確認裝潢完成後，緊接著就是布置展位、擺設展品及依據動線規畫、架設軟和硬體設備。

展覽期：展期通常為期五天，展覽結束後，展商需在主辦單位規定的時間內清空展位，即除了裝潢之外的所有展品及物品等需搬離。對於跨海展覽，花費一筆為數不小的運費將展品運抵展館為不可避免的，因此一般不建議在展覽結束後大費周章的打包展品再運回，最好的方式是以優惠價格銷售給當地或其它海外客戶。

展後期：到海外參展，除了展覽相關費用，參展人員的機票食宿等人事成本也是一筆可觀的開銷，因此可藉此機會在展覽結束後多作停留，順道拜訪當地既有客戶，拉近與客戶關係，當然需在展前即與客戶敲定相關拜訪行程。也有些展商會另外安排觀光旅遊行程。

職場經驗談

綜合上述，參展行程約為期十到十四天，返回工作崗位後，除了補足這兩週來未處理或未完整處理的庶務性工作外，另一個重要的工作就是整理展覽紀錄，排出優先處理順序，進行後續追蹤。完成答應客戶的代辦事項應列在首要，如回覆詢價或提供樣品等。而針對僅索取目錄，無特定代辦事項的客戶，可列在最後，追蹤對方檢視目錄之結果及採購意願。而針對可能啟動交易的目標客戶，可另外安排拜訪行程，積極爭取合作機會。

菜鳥變達人

中翻英練習

1. 電信公司的營業時間應方便客戶。

2. 你方便在本週末前提供報價嗎？

中翻英解答

1 The business hours of Telecom Company should be convenient to clients.

2 Is it convenient for you to offer the quotation by this weekend?

2-2 商務旅行
Business Travel

2-2-1 行程確認
Itinerary Confirmation

★情境說明

Best Corp. confirms the visitation itinerary with Wind Company.

倍斯特公司和微風公司確認拜訪行程。

★角色介紹

（買方）Buyer: Wind Company.

（賣方）Seller: Best International Trade Corp.

情境對話

B: Hey David. It's Wesley calling.	B: 您好，大偉。我是衛斯理。
W: Hi Wesley. I'm just going to send you my agenda, which we would like to go over during my visit to your company.	W: 我正想將前往拜訪貴司期間的議程寄給您

B: What a coincidence! I'm calling to reconfirm your visit itinerary and agenda. You will arrive at TPE Airport Terminal II at 22:35 on Jan. 29 and meet us on Jan. 30 and Feb. 1. After our year-end party on Feb. 1, you will take Eva airline BR0198 on Feb. 2. The flight departure time is 8:50.

B: 真巧！我打電話來就是要再次確認您的訪問日程和議程。您將在一月二十九日抵達臺北機場第二航站，在一月三十日和二月一日與我們會面。在我司二月一日的年終派對之後，您將搭乘二月二日的長榮航空BR0198航班。飛機起飛的時間是上午八點五十分。

W:That's right.

W:沒錯。

B: What time are we exactly going to meet on Jan. 30 and Feb. 1?

B: 我們一月三十日和二月一日的確切會議時間是何時呢？

W:We scheduled to meet at 9:00 a.m. in your office.

W:我們排定在上午九點於貴司的辦公室會面。

B: Got it. I'll send a van for you between the hotel and the company during your stay. And I will drive you to the airport personally on Feb. 2.

B: 瞭解。在您們停留期間，我會派車接送您們往返於酒店及我司。二月二日，我會親自開車送你到機場。

W:Appreciate your arrangement. BTW, please remember to cover the cost reduction issue in the agenda.

W:感謝您的安排。對了，請記得在討議程中加入價格調降議題。

B: Yes. I have written it down in my note.

B: 好的。我已記在我的筆記本中。

W:Great. I'm looking forward to seeing you. Ciao.

W:太好了。期待見到您。再見！

關鍵字彙

go over *(ph.)* [go ˈovɚ] **察看、翻閱**

同義詞 review, examine, study

相關詞 go over a schedule 察看時間表；go over the books 察看帳本

coincidence *(a.)* [ko`ɪnsədənt] **符合的、巧合的**

同義詞 corresponding, correspondent, concurring

相關詞 be merely coincident 純屬巧合；be coincident with the fact 與事實相符

itinerary *(n.)* [aɪ`tɪnəˌrɛrɪ] **旅程、路線**

同義詞 travel route, travel plans, travel journal

相關詞 other scenic spots than those on the itinerary 行程外的景點

terminal *(n.)* [`tɝmən!] **航空站、總站、終點**

同義詞 bus / train station

相關詞 bus terminal 公車總站；terminal stage 末期

departure time *(ph.)* [diˈpɑ:tʃə taim] **出發時間，起飛時刻**

同義詞 checkout time；time of departure

相關詞 departure time on schedule 準時起飛；actual depature time 實際起飛時間

exactly *(adv.)* [ɪg`zæktlɪ] **確切地，完全地**

同義詞 precisely, in every way, indeed

相關詞 exactly so 確實如此；not exactly 並沒有

關鍵句型

further to A's letter to B (on date) 提及A在某日發函給B

例句說明

Further to Janet's earlier **letter to you on Jan. 1st,** she would drop you by next week.

➡ 提及珍妮特一月一日發函予您，她將在下週去拜訪您。

Further to your previous **letter to me on Jan. 1st** about the shipment postponement, we can only accept the one week later.

➡ 提及您一月一日發函予我，我司僅可接受延遲一週。

替換句型

Referring to your previous letter of Jan. 1st informing shipment postponement, we can only accept one week later.

as sb. be well aware that… 如某人清楚所知

例句說明

As you were well aware that the shipment of your order will be postponed one week later.

➡ 如您清楚所知，貴司訂單將延遲一週出貨。

As you were well aware by Janet's email that she will drop you by next week.

➡ 如您由珍妮特的信函得知，她將在下週去拜訪您

替換句型

As you can tell by Janet's email that she will drop by you next week.

勵志小格言

You'll never achieve 100 percent if 99 percent is okay."

~ By Will Smith, Actor

如果 99% 已經足夠，你永遠不會到達 100%。 *～演員　威爾史密斯*

英文書信這樣寫

Dear Wesley,

Further to my letter to you on Dec. 1st, as you were well aware that my CEO and I will take part in your year-end party.

We'll arrive at TPE Airport Terminal II on Jan. 29th at 22:35 taking the Eva airline BR0011 and spend the night in Taipei. The next morning we will be heading for your company and spend two days for project discussion, and attend your party on Feb 1st. Our plan is to leave for Tokyo on Feb. 2nd. With attached please refer to our fright schedule.

I would appreciate it very much if you could reserve both Taipei and Taichung hotels for us. Besides, please suggest the proper transportation we can take to get to the hotel and your city.

Thanks a lot for your big favor.

Yours sincerely,
David Brad

中文翻譯

衛斯理您好：

提及我在十二月一日寄給您的信文，相信您已清楚我司執行長將與我一同參加貴司的年終尾牙派對。

我們將搭乘長榮航空 BR0011 航班，於一月二十九日抵達臺北國際機場第二航站，並於當晚在臺北過夜。第二天早上，我們將前往貴司，預計兩天時間討論新專案及參觀貴司工廠，而後於二月一日參加貴司派對。我們的計畫是在二月二日啟程到東京。詳細請參考附件航班表。

如您能為我們預定在臺北和台中的酒店，我們將不勝感謝。此外，請建議前往酒店及貴城市的適當交通工具。

十分感激您的大力協助。

大衛布萊德　敬啟

知識補給

在外交場合中，「握手」是見面時主要的禮儀，不論是在表達謝意、恭賀、或者慰問等的場合，握手可說是適用於絕大多是國家。因應國情及文化差異，各國也有不同的見面禮節，比較為大家熟悉的有日本的鞠躬禮，鞠躬彎腰的度數與對方的輩分位階有關，由最高到同輩份依序是45˚、30˚以及15˚。而歐美國家常見的有擁抱，向右左側依序擁抱一次；吻手，對象為男士親吻女士的手背；親吻，同樣依輩份不同親吻方式也有所差異，但一般來說是以互貼右左側臉頰為主。

職場經驗談

需特別注意的是即便擁抱、吻手及親吻是歐美國家常見的外交禮儀，但面對較不熟悉或者初次見面的對象仍建議以握手為主。除非對方是長期合作且關係密切的合作夥伴，則另當別論。

菜鳥變達人

中翻英練習

1. 提及供應商上週來函，原物料價格已上漲。

---

2. 如製造商清楚由供應商的信文得知，原物料價格上漲是勢在必行。

中翻英解答

1 Further to supplier's letter to me last week, the raw material prices have risen.

2 As manufacturers were well aware by supplier's email last week, the rise in materials costs is imperative.

2-2-2 簽證申請 Applying for Visa

★情境說明

ABC Co. requests invitation letter from Best Corp. to apply for visa.

ABC公司要求倍斯特公司提供邀請函以申請簽證。

★角色介紹

（買方）Buyer: ABC Co., Ltd.

（賣方）Seller: Best International Trade Corp.

情境對話

B: Best Corp. This is Linda. How may I help you?

B: 倍斯特公司，我是琳達。需要甚麼協助嗎？

A: Hello Linda, this is Olivia Porter from ABC Co. Is Wesley available?

A: 你好，琳達。我是ABC公司的奧利維亞波特。衛斯理有空嗎？

B: Mr. Yang is in the meeting right now.

B: 楊先生現正在會議中。

A: What time should I ring him again?

A: 我應該什麼時候再打給他呢？

B: I'm not quite sure, as he will be at dinner with domestic suppliers after meeting. Would you like to leave a message?

B: 我不是很確定，他在會議後與國內供應商有個飯局。您想留個口信嗎？

A: Well… OK. I'm going to attend the trade show in Shanghai and would drop in on your Shanghai office. I'd like to ask an invitation letter to apply for China Visa. The hardcopy of my passport was just sent to Wesley's email box few minutes ago.

A: 嗯…好吧。我要去參加上海的貿易展，並順道拜訪貴公司上海辦事處。我想要一封邀請函申請中國簽證。我在幾分鐘前寄了我的護照影本到衛斯理的郵箱。

B: Okay, I have written it all down and will make sure Mr. Yang gets the message.

B: 好的，我已經寫下來了，並確定會讓楊先生收到這個訊息。

A: Thank you so much. Linda.

A: 太感謝您了，琳達。

B: Any time.

B: 不客氣。

關鍵字彙

domestic *(a.)* [də`mɛstɪk] **國內的**

同義詞 internal; civil

相關詞 domestic economy 國內經濟；domestic flight 國內航線

drop in *(ph.)* [drɔp in] **順道拜訪、突然來訪**

同義詞 drop by, come by, look in

相關詞 drop in on sb. 偶然拜訪某人

apply for *(ph.)* [əˈplai fɔ:] **申請**

同義詞 put in for；make an application for

相關詞 apply for a passport 申請護照；apply for a position 謀職

關鍵句型

Sth. will be borne by sb. 某事物費用由某人承擔

例句說明

The return shipping will be borne by the seller.

➡ 退貨費用將由賣方承擔。

The exhibition fee and all relevant expenses will be borne by the joint exhibitors on an equal footing.

➡ 參展費用及所有相關花費將由聯合展商平均負擔。

替換句型

The return shipping will be at seller's expense.

勵志小格言

The time is always right to do what is right.

~ By Dr. Martin Luther King

做對的事永遠都是時候。 *～民運領袖 馬丁 路德金恩 博士*

英文書信這樣寫

Main Office - Best Corp. in Shanghai, Mainland China
1 Nanjing Road East Shanghai, Shanghai 200001, China
Tel: 86-21-1111-1111 / Email: best.shoffice@best.com

INVITATION LETTER

To whom it may concern:

It's our great honor to invite Ms. Olivia Porter of ABC Co., Ltd. to visit the main office of Best Group in Shanghai to discuss our future cooperation plan. Her business trip will start from March 1st, 2015 to March 14th, 2015. To strengthen and develop the trade relations between both sides in the future, Ms. Olivia Porter will come to China many times. Please grant Ms. Olivia Porter the necessary privileges to obtain a Multiple Visa to visit China. Her personal details are listed as below:

Name: Olivia Porter / Date of birth: 1st JAN, 1969

Citizenship: the United States of America (U.S.A.) / Passport #: C000111

Please note that during Ms. Poter's stay in China, Best Group does not assume any legal or financial responsibility. All relevant expenses of her visitation will also be borne by her company.

We greatly appreciate your assistance in prompt processing the necessary document to Ms. Porter.

Yours sincerely,
Best Group
1st Jan, 2015

中文翻譯

辦公室 - 倍斯特公司，位於中國上海
中國上海，上海南京東路1號，郵遞區號 200001
電話：86-21-1111-1111／電郵：best.shoffice@best.com

邀請函

敬啟者：

我們很榮幸地邀請ABC有限公司的奧利維亞・波特小姐參觀倍斯特集團在上海的主要辦公室，討論雙方未來合作計畫。她出差期間將從西元二零一五年三月一日開始至西元二零一五年三月十四日止。為鞏固和發展雙方未來貿易關係，奧利維亞・波特小姐將會來訪中國多次。請給予必要的權限，賦予奧利維亞波特小姐訪問中國的多次簽證。她的個人資訊如下：

姓　　名：奧利維亞・波特
出生日期：西元一九六九年一月一日
國　　籍：美國
護照號碼：C000111

請注意，波特小姐在中國停留期間，倍斯特集團不承擔任何法律和財務責任。她訪問期間的所有相關的費用也將由她所屬公司承擔。

我們非常感謝您的協助與及時辦理波特小姐所需的文件。

倍斯特集團　敬啟
西元二零一五年一月一日

知識補給

外籍人士申請中國貿易商務簽證（M簽證）除須規定有效期為6個月以上護照、簽證申請表及照片等外，另需提供中國境內商務合作夥伴所出具的商務活動證明檔，通常是出具邀請函件，該邀請函須包含被邀請者個人資訊（姓名、性別、出生日期等）、訪問資訊（入境事由、訪問期間、訪問地點、邀請單位、費用歸屬等）、以及邀請單位資訊（邀請單位名稱、電話、地址、單位用印、法定代表及其簽章等）。另需特別注意被邀請人個人資料需與護照所列一致。

職場經驗談

每次申請簽證皆需依規定出示上述所列相關檔，一般會建議客戶申請六個月（簽證時效六個月）或一年多次簽證（即一年內可出入中國境內多次），因此可將此需求載明在邀請函內。

菜鳥變達人

中翻英練習

1. 請給予新進員工參加年度旅遊的全額補助。

2. 年度旅遊費用將由公司支付。

中翻英解答

1 Please grant the new employees full subsidy to join the annual traveling.

2 The annual traveling expenses will be borne by the company.

2-2-3 代訂航班
Flight Booking

★情境說明

ABC Co. requests Best Corp. sharing flight information.

ABC公司需求倍斯特公司提供航班訊息。

★角色介紹

（買方）Buyer: ABC Co., Ltd.

（賣方）Seller: Best International Trade Corp.

情境對話

A: Olivia speaking.

A: 我是奧利維亞。

B: Hello, Olivia. This is Wesley from Best Corp. I were sorry to miss your call yesterday.

B: 你好，奧利維亞。我是倍斯特公司的衛斯理。很抱歉昨天錯過您的來電。

A: Don't say so.

A: 快別這麼說。

B: The hardcopy of our invitation letter was just emailed to you. Please check the details, especially your personal

B: 我司的邀請函副本剛剛以電子郵件發送給您。請檢查函中細節，特別

data. The formal one will be sent out to you once confirmed.

是您的個人資料。一旦您確認無誤，正式函件將郵寄給您。

A: I'll. Appreciate your promt response. One more thing, one friend will meet me in Shun De to tour Hong Kong together. Do we need a reservation to go Hong Kong by ferry? What's the fare for a round trip ticket?

A: 我會的。感謝你的即時回覆。還有一件事，一位朋友將和我在順德會合，並一起旅遊香港。我們去香港的渡輪需要預約嗎？往返票價是多少？

B: Which terminal of Hong Kong?

B: 香港的哪一個碼頭？

A: It should be China Ferry Terminal.

A: 應該是中港城碼頭。

B: Not a problem. I will email you the ferry schedule and fare table before leaving the office. It's not suggested to book the flight ticket in advance unless you can be sure the departure time.

B: 沒問題。我會在下班前電郵渡輪時間表和票價表給您。我不建議提前預訂船票，除非您能確定出發的時間。

關鍵字彙

reservation *(n.)* [ˌrɛzɚ`veʃən] 預定（飯店、交通工具、席位等）

同義詞 ordering in advance, advance booking, retaining

相關詞 reservation service 預約服務；reservation park 保留地

ferry *(n.)* [`fɛrɪ] 渡輪、渡口

同義詞 ferryboat, boat

相關詞 ferryman 渡船夫；ferry service 渡輪服務

round trip *(ph.)* 往返旅行

同義詞 two-way trip

相關詞 round trip time 往返時間；round trip ticket 來回票；one way ticket 單程票

關鍵句型

Sb. hereby V. … 特此/謹此…..

例句說明

I hereby express my appreciation to your company.

➡ 謹此向貴公司致上謝意。

The buyer was offended by the seller's late response again and again, and **hereby requested** a formal apology.

➡ 買方因賣方一而再再而三的延遲回覆感到氣憤，特此要求正式道歉。

替換句型

This is to express my appreciation to your company.

勵志小格言

Read over and over, meaning comes out.

~ From History of the Three Kingdoms

書讀百遍，其義自見。

~《三國誌》

英文書信這樣寫

Dear Olivia,

I'm hereby sending you the below fare and time table of ferry transiting between Shun De Port and China Ferry Terminal as request. I hope it will be helpful to you.

Route	From Hong Kong		From Port	
	Departure	Schedule	Arrival	Schedule
Shun De	China Ferry Terminal	08:30	China Ferry Terminal	08:30
		11:00		09:30
		13:30		11:00
		15:20		15:00
		18:00		18:00
	Hong Kong Town To Shun De		Shun De To Hong Kong Town	
	Adult	Child (Ages 1 to under 5)	Adult	Child (Ages 1 to under 5)
VIP	HKD295	HKD185	HKD295	HKD185
First Class	HKD275	HKD170	HKD275	HKD170
Economy	HKD240	HKD155	HKD240	HKD155

If you have any further requirements, please feel free to contact me at any time.

Wishing you a wonderful trip to China!

Yours sincerely,

Wesley Yang

中文翻譯

奧莉維亞您好：

依據您的需求，特此提供下列往返順德港和中港城運碼頭之間的渡輪費用和船班表。希望能對你有所幫助。

航線	離港		抵港	
	出發碼頭	開航時間	抵達碼頭	開航時間
順德港	中港城碼頭	08:30	中港城碼頭	08:30
		11:00		09:30
		13:30		11:00
		15:20		15:00
		18:00		18:00
	香港市區　至　順德港		順德港　至　香港市區	
	成人	小童（1-5歲以下）	成人	小童（1-5歲以下）
特等位	HKD295	HKD185	HKD295	HKD185
頭等位	HKD275	HKD170	HKD275	HKD170
普通位	HKD240	HKD155	HKD240	HKD155

如有任何進一步需求，請隨時與我聯繫。祝你有個美好的中國之旅！

衛斯理　楊　敬啟

知識補給

因應網際網路的普及運用，現階段國內各大眾運輸系統班次訊息取得已相當便捷，只要能確定運輸工具種類及起訖點，基本上國外客戶欲搭乘國內交通大眾運輸工具只要至其網站即可查詢到航班表，甚至可完成線上預訂作業。但大多數客戶對它國大眾運輸系統不甚熟悉，最佳的方式是我方主動提供相關資訊供客戶參考。

職場經驗談

需特別注意有些國內大眾運輸系統可能因尖峰離峰時段差異，會出現一票難求之情形。因此在能確定起訖時間及地點的狀況下，我方可事先協助客戶預訂及購買票券。

菜鳥變達人

中翻英練習

1. 不建議在通過功能性測試前使用替代材質。

---

2. 你在此被委派為我司在東京市的業務代表。

中翻英解答

1 It's not suggested to use substitute materials without success of performance testing.

2 You are hereby appointed as our sales representative in Tokyo.

2-2-4 交通安排 Transportation Arrangement

★情境說明

ABC Co. requests Best Corp. sharing transportation information.

ABC公司需求倍斯特公司提供交通訊息。

★角色介紹

（買方）Buyer: ABC Co., Ltd.

（賣方）Seller: Best International Trade Corp.

情境對話

B: Hello, Olivia. This is Wesley Yang from Best Co.

B: 您好，奧利維亞。我是倍斯特公司的衛斯理楊。

A: Hello, Wesley. Thank you for the invitation letter of your year-end party. It's my pleasure to attend the party.

A: 您好，衛斯理。謝謝您的年終派對邀請函。我很榮幸能參加派對。

B: Great to hear that. Is your itinerary done?

B: 很高興聽到這個消息。您的行程確定了嗎？

A: Not really. I'm in contact with some other suppliers in Asia to consolidate the final schedule. Before that, I need your suggestion of transportation so that I can take to get to your place from airport.

B: I will send a van to meet you at the airport.

A: You don't need to do that. I'd love to take public transport and enjoy the scenery along the way.

B: Well, high speed rail is a good choice. I can share you with the THSR timetable of your flight arrival date. Is it necessary to reserve a room for you?

A: Thanks for asking. I can deal with it on my own.

B: All right then, please never hesitate to let me know any further requirement any time, OK?

A: I will. My dear friend.

A: 不全然是。我正與亞洲其他一些供應商聯繫，以整合最終的時間表。在那之前，我需要您建議可以到達貴公司的交通工具。

B: 我可以派車去機場接你。

A: 不需要這樣做。我喜歡搭乘公共交通工具欣賞沿途的風景。

B: 那麼高速鐵路是一個不錯的選擇。我可以提供您航班到達當日的高鐵時間表。需要為你訂房間嗎？

A: 感謝您詢問。我可以自己處理。

B: 那好吧，任何時間有任何進一步需求，請不要客氣讓我知道，好嗎？

A: 我會的，我親愛的朋友。

關鍵字彙

consolidate *(v.)* [kən`sɑlə͵det] **統一、整頓**

同義詞 unify, merge, integrate

相關詞 consolidated financial statement 合併財務報表；consolidated interest rate 綜合利率

get to *(ph.)* **抵達；把…送到**

同義詞 arrive at, arrive in, reach

相關詞 get to the point 說到要點；get to the bottom of Sth. 弄清某事的真相

public transport *(ph.)* [ˈpʌblik trænsˈpɔ:t] **公共運輸**

同義詞 mass transit, transportation system

相關詞 public transport facilities 公共交通設施；public administration 公共管理

choice *(n.)* [tʃɔɪs]

同義詞 option, selection, pick

相關詞 have no choice 迫不得已；multiple-choice 有多項選擇的

timetable *(n.)* [`taɪm͵tebl̩] **時刻表**

同義詞 schedule, list, program

相關詞 schedule timetable 課表；travel timetable 行程表

deal with *(ph.)* [di:l wið] **對待、處理**

同義詞 trade with, handle, take care of

相關詞 deal with complaints 處理客訴；deal with problem 解決問題

關鍵句型

A be in contact with B… A與B聯繫關於…

例句說明

The buyer is in daily video **contact with the seller** to follow up the production progress.

➡ 買方每天視訊聯繫賣方追蹤生產進度。

Jack is always in direct contact **with the customer** by phone call about shipping schedule.

➡ 傑克通常直接電話聯繫客戶出貨事宜。

替換句型

Jack always communicates with the customer by phone call directly about shipping schedule.

Sb. take care of sth. on one's own 某人自行處理某事

例句說明

The manufacturers must take care of the product inspection on their own before releasing.

➡ 製造商在出貨前須自行安排產品檢驗。

You have to take care of the shipping schedule on your own.

➡ 你必須自行處理出貨排程。

替換句型

You have to deal with the shipping schedule by yourself.

英文書信這樣寫

Dear Olivia

I hereby acknowledge receipt of your itinerary and well noted that you will take care of the hotel reservation on your own.

Per your requirement, please refer to the suggested timetable from Taoyuan to Taichung as below. Or, you can go to THSR website on http://www5.thsrc.com.tw/en/ for more details.

Train I.D.	Remark	Departure Time	Arrival Time	Adult	Children Senior Disabled	Group Ticket
763		22:15	22:52	NT$590	NT$295	NT$560
399		22:31	23:01	NT$590	NT$295	NT$560
541		22:52	23:30	NT$590	NT$295	NT$560
545		23:22	23:59	NT$590	NT$295	NT$560

Shall there be anything I can do for you, please never hesitate to contact me. I look forward to seeing you soon.

Yours sincerely,
Wesley Yang

中文翻譯

奧利維亞您好：

特此告知收到您的行程，並已知悉您將自行處理酒店預訂事宜。

依據您的要求，請參考建議的桃園至台中之班次時間表如下。或者，您可以直接上高鐵網站http://www5.thsrc.com.tw/en/ 獲知詳情。

班次	備註	出發時間	抵達時間	全票	半票 優待票	團體票
763		22:15	22:52	NT$590	NT$295	NT$560
399		22:31	23:01	NT$590	NT$295	NT$560
541		22:52	23:30	NT$590	NT$295	NT$560
545		23:22	23:59	NT$590	NT$295	NT$560

如有任何我司可以為您效勞的地方，請不要客氣聯絡我。期待儘速見到您。

衛斯理楊　敬啟

勵志小格言

Our greatest glory consists not in never falling but in rising every time we fall.

~ By Oliver Goldsmith

我們最值得自豪的不在於從不跌倒，而在於每次跌倒之後都爬起來。

～奧利弗 · 哥德史密斯。

知識補給

英文書信中常用的直述感謝詞句：

We are / feel eternally grateful to you for your support and assistance.

We are / feel particularly thankful to you for your support and assistance.

We are / feel very much obliged by your support and assistance.

We are / feel deeply indebted to your support and assistance.

職場經驗談

表達感謝的語句口語上多數以「Thank」，及「Appreciate」居多，需注意的一點是「thank」當作動詞（v.）時，其後接感謝的對象，而後加上介係詞 for 及感謝的事項，即thank + sb. + for sth.，例句：We thank you for your assistance.；而「appreciate」當作動詞（v.）時，其後可直接加上 sb. 或 sth.，例句：We appreciate your assistance 或 We appreciate you.

菜鳥變達人

中翻英練習

1. 小組成員必須透過即時通訊軟體互相交流最新出貨進度。

2. 莉迪亞會自行處理這件事。

中翻英解答

1 Group members have to be in contact with each other through line to share updated shipping status.

2 Lydia will take care of this matter on her own.

2-2-5 食宿預定
Restaurant & Hotel Reservation

★情境說明

Best Corp. makes hotel reservation for customer.

倍斯特公司替客戶代訂飯店。

★角色介紹

（飯店）Hotel: Sheraton Grande Taipei Hotel

（賣方）Seller: Best International Trade Corp.

情境對話

H: Sheraton Grande Taipei Hotel. This is Max. How may I help you?

H: 臺北喜來登酒店。我是馬克斯。有什麼需要我幫忙的嗎？

B: Hello. I'd like to book two single rooms for my clients.

B: 您好，我想替客戶訂兩間單人房。

H: For what date, please?

H: 訂哪一天呢？

B: January 28 of next year. One night.

B: 明年一月二十八日，一個晚上。

H: Sure, sir. We have deluxe room at NTD 6,900 and premier room at NTD 7,400. Both types are king size.

H: 好的，先生。我們有豪華客房，房價台幣6900元，及行政客房，房價為台幣7400元。兩種房型都是加大床。

B: Is the breakfast included in the rate?

B: 房價包含早餐嗎？

H: Yes, and tax plus.

H: 是的，而且是含稅價。

B: OK, two premier rooms.

B: 好的，訂兩個房間。

H: Client's name, please.

H: 請說客戶的姓名。

B: Mr. David Brad and Mr. William Ryder.

B: 大衛布拉德 先生和威廉瑞德 先生。

H: Ok, sir. Your rooms are reserved.

H: 好的，先生，房間已預訂。

B: Please email the reservation letter to best.headquarter@best.com.tw

B: 請電郵訂房確認書到best.headquarter@best.com.tw

H: No problem, sir.

H: 沒問題，先生。

B: BTW, is the meal available whole day?

B: 對了，飯店整天供餐嗎？

H: The restaurants close at 10:00 a.m., but the hotel offers 24-hour room service.

H: 餐館在晚上10:00關閉，但飯店提供24小時客房服務。

B: I see. Thank you.

B: 瞭解了。謝謝您！

H: My pleasure.

H: 不客氣。

關鍵字彙

book *(v.)* [bʊk] **預定、預約**

同義詞 reserve, order in advance

相關詞 book in 登記；book oneself a flight 為自己訂機票

single room *(ph.)* [ˈsiŋgl ru:m] **單人房**

同義詞 single bedroom, single bed

相關詞 double room / twin room 雙人房；suite 套房（一般指含客廳的房型）；extra bed 加床

pick sb. up *(ph.)* **以車搭載某人**

同義詞 drive sb., carry sb.

相關詞 pick up with sb. 結識某人；pick oneself up 跌倒後起來

organize *(v.)* [ˋɔrgəˏnaɪz] **組織、安排**

同義詞 arrange, set up, establish

相關詞 organized tour 團體旅遊；organized labor 隸屬工會的人

關鍵句型

A meet B at/in some place A 與B在某地會面

例句說明

I tend to **meet you in the hotel restaurant** to discuss the project details over the lunch.

➡ 我想與你在飯店餐廳會面，在席間邊吃邊談專案細節。

Shall **I meet you in the hotel lobby** directly?

➡ 我可以直接在飯店大廳接妳嗎？

替換句型

Shall I go to the hotel lobby to meet you directly?

勵志小格言

I have decided to be happy, because it is good for my health. *~ By French Writer Voltaire*

我要做個快樂的人，因為它對我的健康有好處。 *～法國作家　伏爾泰*

英文書信這樣寫

Dear David,

I were delighted to receive your itinerary and have arranged the hotel reservation according to your requirements as below. Please also find attached hotel reservation letters.

Date	Jan. 28th	Jan. 29th ~ Feb. 1st
Hotel	Sheraton Grande (in Taipei)	Windsor Hotel (in Taichung)
Room Type	Premier Room / King Bed	Deluxe Room / King Bed
	* no smoking	* no smoking
	* w/ breakfast	* w/ breakfast

We will send a van to pick you up from TPE airport to Sheraton Grande Taipei Hotel on Jan. 28th. Next morning our CEO and I will meet you personally on 9:00 am at the hotel and organize a welcome dinner for you that night. On the last day, said Feb. 2nd, the van will drive you to the airport by 6:00am.

Please feel free to let me know for any need during your staying. I look forward to seeing both of you.

Yours sincerely,
Wesley Yang

中文翻譯

大偉您好：

很高興收到您的行程，並已根據您的要求預訂酒店如下。同時附上附件訂房確認書。

日期	一月二十八日	一月二十九日 至 二月一日
飯店	臺北喜來登酒店	台中裕元花園酒店
房型	行政客房/ 加大床	豪華客房 / 加大床
	* 非吸菸房	* 非吸菸房
	* 含早餐	* 含早餐

我司將於一月二十八日派車接您們從桃園國際機場到臺北喜來登酒店。第二天早上，我司執行長和我將親自在早上九點到飯店接您們，並於當天晚上為您們舉辦歡迎晚宴。最後一天，即二月二日，我們的車會在早上六點前開車送您們到機場。

在您們停留期間如有任何需要，請隨時讓我知道。期待見到二位。

衛斯理　楊　敬啟

知識補給

其它訂房常用詞彙：

What kind of room type, please?

How many days will you stay?

The price / fee includes breakfast, tax and service charge.

What is the room charge / fee / price for a deluxe room per night?

How much is the room per night?

Do you have any vacancies tonight?

Do you have a room available for tonight?

I'd like a room with a seaside / hill view for two days starting next Friday.

職場經驗談

協助客戶訂房後可將飯店的訂房確認書或訂房號碼提供予客戶，以便加快飯店辦理客戶入住登記時之查詢流程，使客戶在經歷舟車勞頓後，能順利且快速地下榻飯店休息。

菜鳥變達人

中翻英練習

1. 知道在大地震後你們都安然無恙，我的每一位成員真切感到開心。

2. 奧莉維亞上週在紐約甘迺迪機場偶遇衛斯理。

中翻英解答

1 Everyone in my team is truly delighted to know all you are well after big earthquake.

2 Olivia met Wesley in New York Kennedy Airport by chance last week.

2-3 客戶來訪
Visitation

2-3-1 人員介紹
Introduction of Company Staff

★情境說明

Best Corp. introduces company staff to the new customer.
倍斯特公司向新客戶介紹公司人員

★角色介紹

（新客戶）New Customer: Wind Company
（賣方）Seller: Best International Trade Corp.

情境對話

B : I'd like you to meet my general manager, Paul Chen.

B：我想向您介紹我司的總經理，陳保羅。

B : Sir, this is Mr. David Brad from Wind Company.

B：長官，這位是微風公司的布萊德先生。

B : Mr. Brad, I have long been expecting forward to seeing you.

B：大衛布萊德先生，我期待見到您很久了。

W:Mr. Chen, it's a great honor to be here and meet you in person.

W：陳先生，備感榮幸能在這親自見到您。

B :I hope you enjoy the visit to our company.

B：希望您享受此次參訪我司的行程。

W:Thank you.

W：謝謝您！

B :The Business Department is on the second floor. I'd like to introduce you to the sales representative in charge of your company business.

B：業務部在三樓。我想向您介紹負責貴司業務的業務代表。

B :This is Maggie Wang, the senior overseas sales representative in Best Co. She is mainly responsible for EU market.

B：這位是瑪姬王，倍斯特公司的資深海外業務代表，主要負責歐洲市場。

B :I am honored to meet you, Mr. Brad.

B：見到你是我的榮幸，布萊德先生。

W:Charmed to see you, too, Ms. Wang. I am extremely grateful for your help of smoothing our initial cooperation.

W：王小姐，我也很榮幸見到您。非常感激您的協助使我們首次合作順利進行。

B :Not at all. It's my pleasure.

B：不客氣，這是我的榮幸。

關鍵字彙

meet *(v.)* [mit] 見面

同義詞 see

相關詞 meet by chance 不期而遇；meet with a rebuff 碰釘子

in person *(ph.)* 親自、本人

同義詞 personally

相關詞 in the person of 代表，以...身分；to visit in person 親自參訪

in charge of *(ph.)* 負責

同義詞 responsible for

相關詞 in charge of the case 負責此案；in charge of the administration 負責行行政工作

senior *(a.)* [`sinjɚ] 資深的

同義詞 experienced, elder

相關詞 senior official 長官；senior partner 大股東

overseas *(a.)* 海外

同義詞 abroad, external

相關詞 overseas commerce 海外貿易；overseas market 海外市場

sales representative *(ph.)* 業務代表

同義詞 sales delegate, sales negotiator

相關詞 chief representative 首席代表；representative office 代表處

關鍵句型

Sb. be grateful for… 感謝某事

例句說明

I should be grateful if you would send out the sample at an early date.

➡ 如能早日寄出樣品，將不勝感激。

I am grateful for your advice.

➡ 感謝您的忠告。

替換句型

I am indebted for your advice.

I am obliged for your advice.

I am thankful for your advice.

勵志小格言

Vision without action is a daydream. Action without vision is a nightmare.

~ Japanese Proverb

沒有行動的願景是個白日夢。沒有願景的行動是個夢魘。 *～日本諺語*

英文書信這樣寫

Dear Wesley,

I hereby acknowledge receipt of the invitation letter of your year-end party. It's truly a pleasure for me to attend the party.

My plan is to stay in your city for 3 days and spends one day to visit your office for new project discussion. If time permits, I'd also like to tour your plant. The itinerary of my stay will be shared once finalized.

Looking forward to seeing you and your team members in person.

Yours sincerely,
David Brad

中文翻譯

衛斯理您好：

特此告知敬收貴司年終派對邀請函。能參加派對實屬榮幸。

我計畫在貴城市停留三日，一日時間拜訪貴司辦公室討論新專案。如果時間許可，我還想參觀貴司工廠。待行程敲定後，將提供予您。

期待親自見到您及你的團隊成員。

大衛布萊德　敬啟

知識補給

出口企業常用職稱中英對照：

【行政／管理】	【業務／行銷／企劃／設計／國貿】
Chairman 總裁	Operational Manager 業務經理
Vice Chairman 副總裁	Business Controller 業務主任
President 董事長	Business Manager 業務經理
Vice President 副董事長	Customer service 客服
General Manager 總經理	Specialist 專員
Vice President 副總經理	Web Master 網站管理專員
Chief Executive Officer 執行長 (CEO)	Marcom 企劃
Chief Financial Officer 財務長 (CFO)	Marketing 行銷
Chief Information Officer 資訊長 (CIO)	Product Marketing 產品行銷

Chief Knowledge Officer 知識長 (CKO)	Public Relations 公關
Chief Operating Officer 營運長 (COO)	Marketing Development Manager 市場開發部經理
Special Assistant 特別助理	Marketing Manager 市場銷售部經理
Factory Chief 廠長	Marketing Staff 市場銷售專員
Factory Sub-Chief 副廠長	Marketing Assistant 銷售助理
Assistant Vice President 協理(A.V.P.)	Marketing Executive 銷售主管
Manager 經理	Marketing Representative 銷售代表
Assistant Manager 副理	【工程／技術／製造／品管】
Junior Manager 襄理	Product Manager 生產部經理
Section Manager 課長	Line Supervisor 生產線主管
Administrative Staff 行政人員	Engineer 工程師
Assistant 助理	Research and Development Engineer 研究開發工程師
Administrative Assistant 行政助理	Mechanical Engineer 機械工程師
【財務／總務／人資／法務】	Production Engineer 產品工程師
Fund Manager 財務經理	Maintenance Engineer 維修工程師
Accounting Manager 會計部經理	Manufacturing Engineer 製造工程師
Accounting Supervisor 會計部主管	Systems Engineer 系統工程師
Accounting 會計	Systems Operator 系統操作員
Accounting Assistant 會計助理	Quality Assurance 品保(QA)
Auditorial 稽核	Quality Control 品管(QC)
General Affairs 總務	Operator 作業員
Personnel Manager人事部經理	Technician 技術員
Human Resources 人力資源 (HR)	Engineering Technician 工程技術員
Legal Advisor 法律顧問	Manufacturing Worker 生產員工
Buyer 採購員	Quality Control Engineer 質量管理工程師

職場經驗談

不論是客戶來訪或外出洽公拜訪客戶，務必要事先使用專用名片夾準備好個人名片，以利在自我介紹時能及時取出名片，避免臨時找不到名片的尷尬場面，而遞交名片時由位階較低至位階較高的順序遞交，雙手遞交名片後再自我介紹個人姓名、所屬部門及職稱。

菜鳥變達人

中翻英練習

1. 十分感謝貴司的報價。

2. 請容許我向您展示我們的新品。

中翻英解答

1 I am really grateful for your offer.

2 Please allow me to demonstrate you our new product.

2-3-2 公司介紹
Tour of Office Building

★情境說明

Best Corp. gives the new customer a tour of office building.
倍斯特公司向新客戶介紹環境

★角色介紹

（新客戶）New Customer: Wind Company.
（賣方）Seller: Best International Trade Corp.

情境對話

B: Let me show you around our office building.	B: 讓我向你展示我司的辦公樓。
B: The first floor of the building is the switchboard. The Accounting Department and Personnel Department are located behind the switchboard.	B: 位於一樓的是總機，會計部及人事部位於總機後方。
B: The Business Department including marketing division, sales division, R&D division, and shipping division are on the second level.	B: 業務部包含行銷課、業務課、研發課、船務課在二樓。

B: Each department has its own meeting room for department meeting and reception for foreign guests. The restroom is in the south side of each floor.

B: 每個部門有專屬會議室，用來進行部門會議及接待外賓。洗手間位於每一樓層的後方。

W: Don't you set up IT Department to solve the computing issue?

W:貴司沒有設立資訊部門解決電腦問題嗎？

B: We outsource all IT-related work.

B: 我們外包所有資訊相關工作。

W: Is there any facility for sport and recreation?

W:有任何運動及娛樂設備嗎？

B: Employee can enjoy the playground, library, amusement room, pantry room, and other welfare and entertainment facilities on the third floor. Let me lead you to the pantry room to have a cup of latte.

B: 員工可享用位於三樓的運動場、圖書室、娛樂室、茶水間等等其他福利及娛樂設施。讓我帶你到茶水間喝杯拿鐵吧！

關鍵字彙

office building *(ph.)* 辦公樓

同義詞 office tower, office block

相關詞 office furniture 辦公傢俱；office equipment 辦公設備

be located *(ph.)* 位於

同義詞 be seated, lie

相關詞 be located in the south side 位於後方；be located in the north side 位於前方

解析 就方位而言，南方在下，就是指後方，北方在上，則指前方。

division *(n.)* [də`vɪʒən] 部門、課

同義詞 section, branch, department

相關詞 information research division 情報室；division manager 部門經理

reception *(n.)* [rɪ`sɛpʃən] 接待

同義詞 to entertain, to receive

相關詞 reception room 接待處；warm reception 熱烈接待

facility *(n.)* [fə`sɪlətɪ] 設施

同義詞 installation

相關詞 controlled facility 保稅區；production facility 生產設備

welfare *(n.)* [`wɛl͵fɛr] 福利

同義詞 well-being

相關詞 welfare department 福利部；welfare work 福利事業

關鍵句型

Sth. be located behind⋯ 某物座落於⋯之後

例句說明

The restroom is located behind the meeting room.

➡ 洗手間位於會議室後方。

The new exhibition hall is just **located behind** the old one.

➡ 新展示廳就坐落在舊展示廳後方。

替換句型

The new exhibition hall just is set behind the old one.

Let me lead sb. to⋯ 讓我引領某人至⋯

例句說明

Let me lead you the way.

➡ 我替你帶路。

Let me lead you to the new exhibition hall.

➡ 讓我引領你到新展示廳。

替換句型

Let me guide you to the new exhibition hall.

英文書信這樣寫

Dear Mr. Brad,

How's everything? It's so glad to learn that you will have a business trip to our country from March 20 to 27. Is it possible for you to arrange an appointment to discuss our initial cooperation plan during your stay here? Besides, I would like to take this opportunity to show you our newly built office building.

If this arrangement is workable, please let me know the potential date convenient for you.

We look forward to your confirmation in soon.

Yours sincerely,
Wesley Yang

中文翻譯

布萊德先生您好：

一切都好嗎？很高興得知你將於三月二十日至二十七日期間出差至我國。在您停留本地期間，是否可能安排會面討論我們的初步合作計畫？另外，我想藉此機會帶您參觀我們的新落成的辦公樓。

如果這個安排可行，請讓我知道您方便的日期。

期盼您儘速確認。

衛斯理　楊　敬啟

勵志小格言

The best way to succeed is to discover what you love and then find a way to offer it to others in the form of service, working hard, and also allowing the energy of the universe to lead you.

~Oprah Winfrey, Talk Show Host

成功的最佳方法是找到自己的所愛，然後找到一個方法，以服務他人的形式，將所愛提供給他人，努力工作，並且允許宇宙的能量來引導你。　*～脫口秀主持人　歐普拉*

知識補給

期盼收到儘速回覆的書信結尾語：

Please reply at your earliest convenience.

Please favor us with your decision as early as possible.

As the matter is urgent, an early reply will be greatly appreciate.

A prompt reply would help us greatly.

An immediate reply would greatly oblige us.

We hope to be favored with a reply at an early date.

We await the pleasure of receiving a favorable reply without delay.

We should be obliged by your immediate reply.

We should appreciate a prompt response.

職場經驗談

國外客戶參訪，若為首次來訪客戶，我方接待人員可先帶領客戶熟悉辦公室環境，並在環境介紹過程中順勢介紹各部門主管，唯介紹業務部門時可一一向客戶介紹相關負責業務組員。環境及人員介紹完畢後，則引領客戶至會議室稍坐片刻，接著可由專人進行公司簡介或欣賞公司簡介影片。最後即進入主題，即會議章程討論。

菜鳥變達人

中翻英練習

1. 讓我引領你會見我的主管。

2. 主管辦公室位於業務部後面。

中翻英解答

1 Let me lead you to meet my supervisor.

2 The supervisor's office is located behind the Business Department.

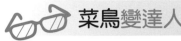

2-3-3 參觀工廠
Factory Tour

★情境說明

Best Corp. gives ABC Co. a facility tour.
倍斯特公司向ABC公司介紹工廠環境

★角色介紹

（買方）Buyer: ABC Co., Ltd.
（賣方）Seller: Best International Trade Corp.

情境對話

B: Let me give you a tour of our facility. The building right behind is factory No. 1. It was set up in 1979.

B: 讓我帶您參觀我們工廠。在身後的這棟建築是一廠，興建於西元1979年。

A: I have learned that you are going to build a new factory.

A: 聽說貴司即將新建新廠。

B: Yes, construction will begin at the end of this year.

B: 是的，將於年底破土動工。

B: Please come this way. On your left is the production area, including casting department, forging department, machining department, polishing department, and QC and packing department. We have four brass gravity casting machines and three low-pressure casting machine. Our production capacity is 700 ton per month.

B: 請往這走。在你左手邊的是生產區包括鑄造部、鍛造部、加工部、拋光部、及品檢包裝部。我們共有四台重力鑄造機及三台低壓鑄造機。我們的月產能是700噸。

A: How many people are working in your factory?

A: 工廠共有多少員工？

B: We have employed over 6,000 workers, but there are many employees earlier returning to their hometown for the coming Chinese New Year.

B: 我們員工超過6000人，但因應即將到來的中國農曆新年，很多員工提前休假返鄉。

A: I see.

A: 了解。

B: Looking to your right side, there are 3 assembly lines. Each line can finish 1000 pieces of the part per hour. We concentrated on FIFO management for WIP, semi-finished or finished product and ERP online. Our

B: 往您的右手邊看去，共有三條裝配線，每條線每小時可完成組裝1000件產品。我們致力於先進先出管理，包括在製品、半成品及成品，及

management and finished products meet the ISO 9001 & ISO 14000 standard.

線上ERP系統。我們的管理及成品符合ISO 9001及ISO 14000標準。

A: I'm really impressed by the well setup of your facility.

A: 哇！對貴司廠區的完善規劃我真是印象深刻。

關鍵字彙

QC *(ph)* 品質控制

相關詞 QA 品質保證

解析 QC（Quality Control）指為達到品質要求，企業內部生產單位所採取的相關檢驗行為。QA（Control Assurance）是企業向自身企業內部或買方所做的品質保證行為。

assembly line *(ph.)* 組裝線

同義詞 production line, line

解析 指由單一生產單位各司其職而後連接起來的連續生產線。主要在於讓單一生產單位只集中處理同一生產製程，而非傳統的讓同一生產單位完整完成一個產品。

FIFO *(ph.)* 先進先出法

相關詞 LIFO 後進先出法

解析 FIFO（First in first out）意指先進倉的貨先賣出去。

WIP *(ph.)* 在製品

相關詞 semi-finished 半成品；finished product 成品

解析 WIP（Work in Process）指正在加工但尚未完成的產品。

semi-finished product *(ph.)* 半成品

同義詞 semi-manufactured goods

解析 指經過一定生產過程並已檢驗合格交付半成品倉庫保管，但尚未製造完工成為成品。

關鍵句型

on one's right / left 在某人右手／左手邊

例句說明

My meeting room is **on your left**.

➡ 我的辦公室在你左手邊。

The showroom is about two meters away **on your right**.

➡ 展示間就在你右手邊約兩公尺遠的地方。

替換句型

The showroom is about two meters away to your right side.

Sb. concentrate on 某人致力於

例句說明

Most of the manufactures **concentrate on** cost reduction.

➡ 多數製造生致力於降低成本。

We concentrate on high quality of product and service.

➡ 我們致力於提供高品質產品及服務。

替換句型

We focus on high quality of product and service.

勵志小格言

Risk comes from not knowing what you're doing

~Warren Buffett, Investor

風險來自於你不知道自己在做什麼。 *～股神　巴菲特*

英文書信這樣寫

Dear Olivia,

I am very pleased to hear that you will visit Taiwan next Monday. Unfortunately, I will be on a business trip to Hong Kong on that day, but will be back that evening.

Whether you are available to stop by Taichung City in Monday afternoon? David Chen, our senior plant director, will be very pleased to take this opportunity to be your tour guide of our Taichung facility. I can meet you to have a cup of coffee at your hotel around 8:00P.M if it's convenient for you.

Please confirm by return if this arrangement is fine for you.

Yours sincerely,
Wesley Yang

中文翻譯

奧莉維亞　您好：

很高興得知您下星期一要造訪臺灣的消息。不巧的是，那天我會出差香港，但當天晚上即會返台。

不知您是否能在星期一下午停留台中？我們的資深廠長大衛 陳非常高興能藉此機會做為您參觀我們台中廠的嚮導。如果您方便的話，我可以約在晚上八點在您下榻的酒店與您會面喝一杯咖啡。

請回覆確認這個安排對您來說是否可行。

衛斯理　楊　敬啟

知識補給

進出口企業常用部門中英文對照:

人事部 Personnel Department
人資部 Human Resources Department
工程部 Engineering Department
行銷部 Marketing Department
企劃部 Planning Department
行政部 Administration Department
技術部 Technology Department
客服部 Service Department

研發部 Research and Development Department(R&D)
秘書室 Secretarial Office
財務部 Financial Department
會計部 Accounting Department
採購部 Purchasing Department
開發部 Product Development Department
業務部 Sales Department
營業部 Business Department
總務部 General Affairs Department

職場經驗談

產品依生產完成度主要區分為成品、半成品和在製品。成品是指已完成全部生產製程，且檢驗合格並入庫，可供銷售的產品；半成品，是指在單一車間已完成加工，且經檢驗合格後入半成品倉，待轉入下一車間繼續加工的產品。在製品，是指仍在單一車間的工序上，正在加工的製品，或雖已加工完畢但尚未檢驗入半成品倉或成品倉的製品。因此在製品是介於原材料和半成品之間，半成品和半成品之間，以及半成品和成品之間的製品。

菜鳥變達人

中翻英練習

1. 我的公司就在這條街的右側。

2. 多數公司致力於擴大國際市場佔有率。

中翻英解答

1 My company is on the right of the street.

2 Most firms concentrate on expanding international market share.

2-3-4 認證稽核
Certification

★情境說明

ABC Co. applies for the certification on Best's parts.

ABC 申請認證倍斯特公司的品項。

★角色介紹

（買方）Buyer: ABC Co., Ltd.
（賣方）Seller: Best International Trade Corp.

情境對話

B: Hello, Olivia. This is Wesley Yang from Best Corp.

B: 你好，奧利維亞。我是倍斯特公司的衛斯理。

A: Bonjour, Wesley. I'm on the point of sending you an email about the IAMPO certification. Your revised documents of Nov. 1st is just confirmed with no doubt by IAMPO.

A: 你好，衛斯理。我正要寄給你關於IAMPO認證的電子郵件。IAMPO剛確認您十一月一日修改的檔案沒有問題。

B: I were concerned about this matter for a whole week.

B: 我整整一週都在擔心這件事。

A: Everything is just ducky so far. The date of certification shall be notified directly to you within these days. Wishing we keep on with such good luck.

A: 目前為止一切都挺好的。這幾天您應該會直接收到認證日期的訊息。希望我們能繼續有這種好運氣。

B: So do I. I'll keep you copied of the certification information on receipt of it.

B: 我也這麼希望。在收到消息後我會知會您。

A: Appreciate.

A: 感謝！

B: Don't mention it. That's what I have to do.

B: 不客氣（快別這麼說）！這是應該的。

關鍵字彙

revise *(v.)* [rɪ`vaɪz] 修改、改編

同義詞 amend, modify, adapt

相關詞 reviser 修訂者；revise the topic 修改主題；revise one's opinions 某人改變其看法

concern *(v.)* [kən`sɝn] 擔心，顧慮

同義詞 care, keep an eye on, worry

相關詞 serious concern 重度關切；remember with concern 掛念

ducky *(a.)* [`dʌkɪ] 挺好的

同義詞 wonderful, very good

相關詞 be just ducky；be quite smooth；be running in smooth 順利

with no doubt *(ph.)* 無庸置疑、斬釘截鐵

同義詞 without doubt, doubtless , undoubted

相關詞 firmly believe without any doubt 堅信；doubtful debt 呆帳

so far *(ph.)* 目前為止

同義詞 up until now, until this moment, thus far

相關詞 so far so good 截至目前為止，一切都很順利；so far as in me lies 竭盡所能

keep on *(ph.)* 繼續保持

同義詞 continue, persist, carry on

相關詞 keep on doing sth. 繼續做某事；keep on one's toe 使某人竭盡心力

關鍵句型

as detailed in the attached (document) 如附(文)詳載

例句說明

You may refer to our working calendar of next year **as detailed in the schedule table**.

➡ 請參閱我司明年度行事曆，詳細如附件行程表。

The inquired piece prices are **as detailed in the attached sheet**.

➡ 所需產品單價如附件詳載。

替換句型

The inquired piece prices are as particularized on the enclosed sheet.

permit me (us) to remind sb. … 容我（我們）提醒某人

例句說明

Permit me to remind the new staff that training will start after lunch.

➡ 容我提醒新人，教育訓練在午餐後開始。

Please **permit us to remind you that** our office will be closed for 5-day-consecutive Christmas' holiday starting from Dec. 23.

➡ 請容我司提醒您，我司辦公室將從十二月二十三日起連休五天聖誕假。

替換句型

Please allow us to call your attention that our office will be closed for 5-day-consecutive Christmas' holiday starting from Dec. 23.

英文書信這樣寫

Dear Wesley,

We enclose here with spread sheet for IAPMO Lead Free Certification. Please fill out yellow highlight areas completely for each size on an individual sheet. As detailed in the attached documents, what we suggested is to list just major components, including the body halves, the ball valve, the stem assembly, and other related matting parts contacting water surface, instead of whole kit. Even though some of these components do not contain lead, but contact water, they still need to be documented.

Permit us to remind you that the required documents should be sent in return by next Monday. Any question, please feel free to let me know.

Yours sincerely,
Olivia Porter

中文翻譯

衛斯理您好：

隨函附上IAPMO無鉛認證表格。請將個別不同尺寸產品的資料完整填寫在各個頁籤的黃色標記區域。如附檔詳載，我司的建議是只列出主要部件包括閥體，閥球，閥杆組件，以及其它會與水接觸的相關配合件，而非完整組裝套件。儘管部分所列元件不含鉛，但會接觸水，因此仍然需要被列表。

容我們提醒您，所須的文件在下週一前寄回所需的文件。如有任何問題，請隨時讓我知道。

奧利維亞　波特　敬啟

勵志小格言

If there is any one secret of success, it lies in the ability to get the other person's point of view and see things from that person's angle as well as from your own.

~By Henry Ford, American automotive entrepreneur

若成功有祕訣，那麼就從自己和他人的觀點來觀看事物。

～美國汽車企業家　亨利．福特

知識補給

IAPMO（美國國際管道暖通機械認證）International Association Plumbing and Mechanical Officials，是美國一個非營利性質的機構。主要從事於建築給排水行業以及建築通風系統之安全使用規範和標準的制訂，並對有關產品進行檢測及認證，包括出版各種安全使用規範UPC、UMC等規範、為從事相關行業的檢驗人員舉辦種類研討會，並頒發檢驗人員資格證書、根據UPC和UMC的要求，對行業內的有關產品給予產品檢驗及認證，以及ISO9000體系認證。

IAPMO是國際管道理事會的重要成員。由於UPC規範在世界上許多國家得到推廣使用，使得IAPMO具有堅實的國際地位。

以上資料來源參考智庫百科網頁http://www.mbalib.com/

職場經驗談

歐美各國客戶十分注重認證（Certification），不論是對產品本身、生產製造流程、製造商人員、生產單位，甚至是出口商及其相關生產業者的社會責任等等。因此在與出口商及其相關生產業者合作前後即可能提出認證需求。依據各產業別不同，所需認證的項目及機構也有所差異，一般來說是由國外客戶向認證機機構提出需求，由出口商及其相關生產業者填具認證機構所需的相關文件後，由國外客戶將相關文件提交予認證機構，而後由認證機構派員至出口商及其相關生產業者進行認證審核，最終依認證合格與否提供稽核報告（Inspection Report），合格者另發給證書（Certificate）。

菜鳥變達人

中翻英練習

1. 所提案之工程建議如附件圖紙詳載。

---

2. 容我提醒您務必準時與會。

中翻英解答

1 The proposal engineering suggestions are as detailed in the attached drawing.

2 Permit me to remind you to be sure to attend the meeting on time.

2-3-5 招待用餐
Entertainment

★情境說明

Best Corp. entertains ABC Co. at dinner.
倍斯特公司招待ABC公司用餐

★角色介紹

（買方）Buyer: ABC Co., Ltd.
（賣方）Seller: Best International Trade Corp.

情境對話

B: Please take your seat and have a look at the menu, Olivia.

B: 請入座看看菜單，奧莉維亞。

A: Thank you. Are there any special dishes you would recommend?

A: 謝謝您。你推薦什麼特別的菜嗎？

B: Peking Roast Duck is the most famous dish at this restaurant. Would you like to try it?

B: 北平烤鴨是這家餐廳最有名的菜。你想嚐嚐看嗎？

A: I've had this dish in China and it was so good.

A: 我曾在中國吃過這道料理，太美味了。

B: The Peking Roast Duck of this restaurant attracts many customers. You must try it.

B: 許多顧客因這家餐廳的北平烤鴨慕名而來。你一定要試試。

A: I'd love to.

A: 我非常樂意。

B: How about the steamed meat dumpling in chili oil（紅油抄手）, the chef's recommendation? Do you like spicy food?

B: 嚐嚐主廚推薦的紅油抄手如何？你吃辣嗎？

A: Any kind of food is fine with me.

A: 我都可以。

B: By the way, it's necessary to prepare knife and fork for you?

B: 對了，需要為您備妥刀叉嗎？

A: There's no need. I can manage chopsticks.

A: 沒有必要。我能用筷子。

B: OK. Let's talk over the dinner.

B: 好吧！那我們邊吃邊談。

關鍵字彙

take a seat *(ph.)* **入座**

同義詞 have a seat，come to the table，be seated

相關詞 lose one's seat 座位被佔；take one's seat 坐在某人座位上；keep one's seat 坐在自己的座位上

recommend *(v.)* [ˌrɛkə`mɛnd] **推薦、建議**

同義詞 speak well of, suggest, advise

相關詞 be highly recommended 大力推薦；be recommended by sb. 某人推薦

famous *(a.)* [`feməs] **著名的、出名的**

同義詞 notable, renowned, well-known

相關詞 world famous 舉世聞名的；famous reputation 盛名

attract *(v.)* [ə`trækt] **吸引**

同義詞 tempt, charm, fascinate

相關詞 attract one's attention 引起某人注意；attracted to sb./sth. 被某人／某事吸引

recommendation *(n.)* [ˌrɛkəmɛn`deʃən] **推薦**

同義詞 proposal, suggestion, advice

相關詞 self-recommendation 自我推薦；recommendation letter 推薦信

manage *(v.)* [`mænɪdʒ] **操縱、使用、達成**

同義詞 control, conduct, handle

相關詞 manage with difficulty 勉強；manage by myself 自己應付

關鍵句型

Would it bother sb. to… 對某人是否方便…？

例句說明

Would it bother your factory to advance our order schedule one week earlier?

➡ 能麻煩貴司工廠把我的訂單排程提前一週嗎？

Would it bother you to meet me at the airport?

➡ 到機場來接我對您來說是否方便？

替換句型

Would it make you in trouble to meet me at the airport?

it be necessary… 做某事是必須的

例句說明

Please let me know if **it's necessary to** meet you at the airport?

➡ 請讓我知道是否需要到機場接您？

The buyer thought **it** would **be necessary to** advance the order schedule one week earlier to catch up with the selling season.

➡ 買方認為將有需要提前一週訂單排程，以趕上銷售季。

替換句型

The buyer felt the necessity to advance the order schedule one week earlier to keep peace with the selling season.

英文書信這樣寫

Dear Wesley,

It was kind of you to invite me to dinner on my arrival date. Unfortunately, I am afraid the dinner date we have set will have to be postponed due to an unexpected schedule change. Would it bother you to rearrange our dinner for the following night?

Please forgive me for any inconvenience it may cause. I look forward to your response soon.

Yours sincerely,
Olivia Porter

中文翻譯

衛斯理您好：

謝謝您邀請我在抵達當日共進晚餐。遺憾的是，恐怕我們約定的晚餐約因為不預期的行程異動而需延期。不知重新安排晚餐到第二天晚上是否方便？

對任何可能造成的不便，敬請見諒。我盼望很快收到你的回覆。

奧莉維亞　波特　敬啟

知識補給

一般中西餐用餐席次安排座位說明圖：

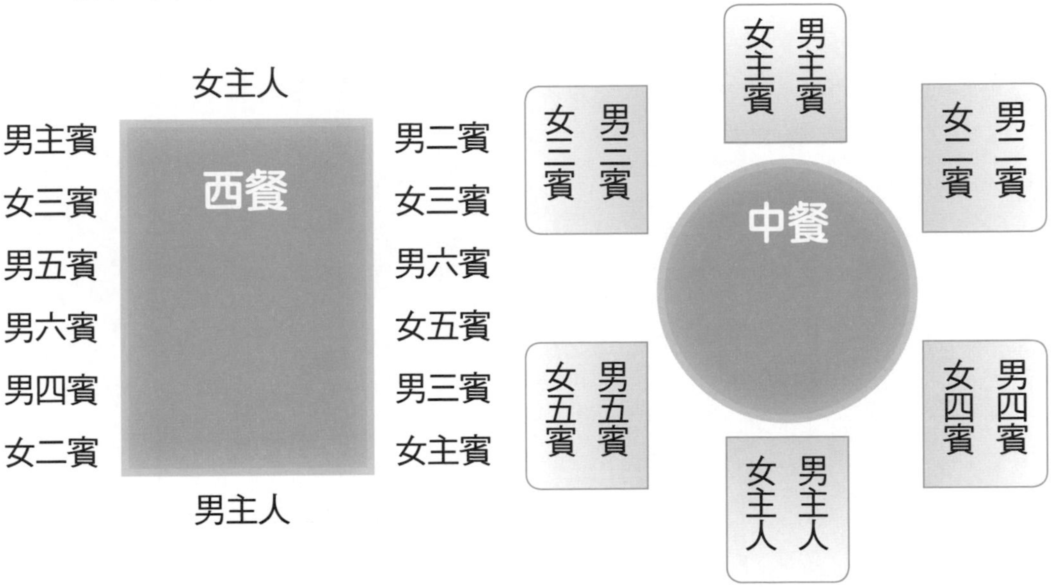

職場經驗談

招待客戶用餐須以客為尊，最好能事先做足功課，瞭解客戶之飲食習慣，尤其是中華料理多煎煮炒炸，口味偏重，並非國外客戶皆能接受，為避免有招待不週之憾，亦可直接於餐前詢問客戶用餐喜好。

3-1 公告通知
Announcement and Notification

3-2 人際互動
Interpersonal Communication

社交公關
Social Intercourse

Part3

3-1 公告通知
Announcement and Notification

3-1-1 活動邀請
Invitation

★情境說明

Best Corp. invites ABC Co. to year-end dinner banquet.
倍斯特公司邀請ABC公司參加年終尾牙。

★角色介紹

（買方）Buyer: ABC Co., Ltd.
（賣方）Seller: Best International Trade Corp.

情境對話

B: Hi, Olivia. I'm calling to invite you to our year-end dinner banquet.

B: 嗨，奧利維亞。我打電話是想邀請你參加我們的尾牙晚宴。

A: Thanks, Wesley. It's my pleasure. We just happen to plan next year's business travel to Asia. When will the

A: 謝謝你，衛斯理。這是我的榮幸。我們碰巧正計畫明年到亞洲的商務

banquet be held? | 旅行。晚宴將會在何時舉行呢？

B: The banquet will take place next Feb 1st.

B: 將在明年二月一日舉行。

A: Sounds good. I should be able to make it.

A: 聽起來不錯，我應該可以參加。

B: Great. Please let me know the number of guests.

B: 太好了。請讓我知道貴司將參加的人數。

A: My general manager will be traveling with me and should also come. Please put us down for two. In case of change, you will be informed in advance.

A: 我司總經理將與我一起出差，應該也會參加晚宴。請登記我們兩位。如果有任何變化，會提前通知您。

B: Sure. Is it necessary for accommodation and transportation arrangement for you?

B: 沒問題。需要為您安排住宿和交通嗎？

A: Please make hotel reservation for us. We're looking forward to staying for two to three days and talking about the cooperation plan of next year. I'll send you our itinerary, once available.

A: 請為我們預訂酒店。我們預計停留兩至三天，並談論明年的合作計畫。待確定後，我會給你我們的行程。

關鍵字彙

invite *(v.)* [ɪn`vaɪt] 邀請

同義詞 welcome, please, ask

相關詞 invitee 被邀請者；invite sb. away 邀某人同行

year-end banquet *(ph.)* 尾牙

同義詞 year-end party, year-end dinner, annual banquet

相關詞 year-end bonus 年終獎金；New Year's Eve 除夕；evening party 晚會

take place *(ph.)* 舉行

同義詞 come off, hold

相關詞 take place as scheduled 如期舉行

guest *(n.)* [gɛst] 賓客

同義詞 customer, visitor

相關詞 unexpected guest 不速之客；guest house 招待所；honored guest 貴賓

put down *(ph.)* 記下；寫下

同義詞 write down, take down, set down

相關詞 put sth. down to 把某項目記在帳上；put sb. down for sth. 預先為某事登記某人

in case of *(ph.)* 假如發生

同義詞 in the event of

相關詞 in the case of 就...來說；in this case 既然這樣

關鍵句型

sb. / sth. just happen to 某人／某事正巧是

例句說明

Nina's traveling date just happens to be the same day as mine.

➡ 妮娜的出差日與我的出差日恰巧是同一天。

Nina just happened to meet me in the exhibition last week.

➡ 妮娜上週在秀展巧遇我。

替換句型

Nina just chanced to meet me in the exhibition last week.

Is it necessary …? 是否需要…？

例句說明

Is it more **necessary** to work an extra shift on Sunday during the peak times of production?

➡ 是否更需要在訂單高峰期安排週日加班？

Is it necessary to arrange airport transfers for you?

➡ 是否需要為您安排機場接送？

替換句型

Do you need any assistance in arranging airport transfers?

勵志小格言

Success is falling nine times and getting up ten.

~Bon Jovi, Singer

成功在失敗了九次後，第十次才獲得。 ～歌手　邦喬飛

英文書信這樣寫

Dear Olivia,

It's my pleasure, on behalf of Best Group to invite you to our company's year-end dinner banquet at Formosa Hotel from 6:00 P.M. to 10:00 P.M. on Friday, Feb. 1st.

Best Group would like to take this opportunity to appreciate your great support to achieve roaring success on business during the year. It would be our great honor if you could attend the party with your family. For your convenience, attached are a map and detailed directions of Formosa Hotel.

Best Group sincerely hopes you can join us at the year-end dinner banquet. Please RSVP if you can come by January 1st, so that we can ensure your place is reserved.

Yours sincerely,
Wesley Yang

中文翻譯

奧莉維亞您好：

謹代表倍斯特集團，很榮幸地邀請您參加我司在二月一日晚上6:00到10:00於福爾摩沙酒店舉辦的年終尾牙晚宴。

倍斯特集團想借此機會感謝您的大力支持，致使我們今年度業務大有斬獲。如您能與您的家人參加晚宴，將是我們的榮幸。為了您的方便，附件為福爾摩沙酒店的地圖及詳細方位。

倍斯特集團真誠地希望您能參加我們的年終宴會。請在一月一日前回覆您是否能前來，以便保留您的座位。

衛斯理　楊　敬啟

知識補給

台灣主要國定假日一般除春節假期之外，其餘均放假一日，每年度相關國定假日排定，可參考行政院人事行政總處網站 http://web.dgpa.gov.tw/mp1.html 之公告及異動。

中華民國開國紀念日（一月一日）
Founding Day of the Republic of China (January 1)
和平紀念日（二月二十八日）
Peace Memorial Day (February 28)
兒童節（四月四日）
Children's Day (April 4)
民族掃墓節（定於清明日）
Tomb Sweeping Day (observed on Qingming Festival).
端午節（農曆五月五日）
Dragon Boat Festival (fifth day of the fifth month of the lunar calendar).
中秋節（農曆八月十五日）
Mid-Autumn Festival (fifteenth day of the eighth month of the lunar calendar).
國慶日（十月十日）
National Day (October 10)
農曆除夕（農曆十二月之末日）
Chinese New Year's Eve (the last day falls of the lunar calendar year).
春節（農曆一月一日至一月三日）
Chinese New Year (first three days of the lunar calendar year).

中國法定節假日清明、端午、中秋、元旦和勞動節各放一天。春節和國慶節各三天，並移動春節及國慶休假時間前後的二個周末四天，稱「倒休」，和法定假期三天集中休假，共計七天時間。而這連續七天休假，即所謂的「黃金週」（Golden Week）又被稱為「長假」。

職場經驗談

尾牙通常會在農曆新年前的一個月內前後舉辦，此時正值歐美地區聖誕假期後所迎接的新第一季度，也是客戶擁有充足出差預算之開始，因此可抓緊機會力邀客戶參加尾牙宴，藉此增進彼此關係，爭取新年度合作方案及訂單。

菜鳥變達人

中翻英練習

1. 我正巧要到印度出差。

---

2. 是否需要安排電話會議做進一步討論？

中翻英解答

1 I just happen to have business travel to India.
2 Is it necessary to set up a conference call for further discussion?

3-1-2 休假公告
Holiday Announcement

★情境說明

Best Corp. notifies ABC Co. of Chinese New Year holiday.
倍斯特公司通知ABC公司有關中國新年休假訊息。

★角色介紹

（買方）Buyer: ABC Co., Ltd.
（賣方）Seller: Best International Trade Corp.

情境對話

B: Hello, Olivia. This is Wesley Yang from Best.

B: 你好，奧利維亞。我是倍斯特的衛斯理 楊。

A: Hey, Wesley. I were just wondering what are you up to lately?

A: 嘿！衛斯理。我正想您最近如何。

B: I were hard pressed to schedule production for coming consecutive holidays. That's also why I'm calling.

B: 為了即將到來的連續假期，我正為了生產排程忙得焦頭爛額。這也是我致電給您的原因。

A: I were communicating with logistic team recently for demand forecast

A: 我最近正與物流部門溝通以取得最新的預估訂

and shipment priority issues, and should work out the forecast order by our Christmas shut down.

單及出貨優先順序，應該在我們的聖誕假期前可擬出預估訂單。

B: Please be reminded to include the demand during our Spring Festival Holiday. You should have received our holiday notice.

B: 請記得包括我們春節假期期間的需求。您應該已收到我司的放假通知。

A: Yeah. The figures have covered it. BTW, could you share me your work calendar of next year?

A: 是的，預估數據已包含春節假期期間的需求。對了，您能提供我貴司明年的行事曆嗎？

B: No problem. I'll email it to you right away after our conversation. Wishing you a happy New Year and having nice Christmas holiday!

B: 沒問題。掛上電話後，我會馬上發電子郵件給您。預祝您新年愉快，並有個美好的聖誕假期。

A: Thanks. Same to you.

A: 謝謝，您也是。

關鍵字彙

consecutive *(a.)* [kən`sɛkjʊtɪv] 連續的

同義詞 sequential, continuous, successive

相關詞 consecutive years 連年；consecutive days 連續日

communicate with *(ph.)* 溝通

同義詞 get in touch with, express thoughts with

相關詞 communicate with each other 互相溝通

logistic team *(ph.)* 物流部門

同義詞 logistic department, operation department

相關詞 logistics company 物流公司；logistics system 物流系統；logistics management 物流管理

shut down *(ph.)* 關閉；停工

同義詞 close down, stop, terminate

相關詞 shut down the plant 工廠停工；shut down the airport 機場關閉

figure *(n.)* [`fɪgjɚ] 數字；數據

同義詞 amount, number, digit

相關詞 huge figure 龐大數目；figure of noise 噪音指數

work calendar *(ph.)* 工作日程

同義詞 job schedule, work schedule

相關詞 public holiday calendar 公休日程表；calendar year 日歷年；lunar calendar 農曆

關鍵句型

Sb. be hard pressed to 某人為⋯ 焦頭爛額；某人膠著於⋯

例句說明

Are you still hard pressed to cutting down the cost of production?

➡ 你仍然膠著於降低生產成本嗎?

Timmy was hard pressed to catch punctual shipment.

➡ 提米為趕上交期而忙得焦頭爛額。

替換句型

Timmy was so bogged down on catching punctual shipment.

Please be reminded to 請謹記某事

例句說明

Please be reminded to send me your holiday notice.

➡ 請記得提供我貴司的休假通知。

Please be reminded to place the order before holiday.

➡ 請記得在休假前下單。

替換句型

Please keep in mind that the order shall be placed before holiday.

英文書信這樣寫

Dear Customers,

This email is to inform you that Best Group will shut down to celebrate the Chinese Lunar New Year. Please refer to the holiday period of worldwide locations as below.

Headquarter - Best International Trade Corp. in Taipei Taiwan

Shut down from Wed. Feb. 18th to Sun. Feb. 22nd

Resume on Mon. Feb. 23rd.

Main Office - Best Corp. in Shanghai, Mainland China

Shut down from Wed. Feb. 18th to Tue. Mar. 5th

Resume on Fri. March 6th.

Delivery Center - Best Inc. in Detroit, Michigan USA

Open as normal business hours between 9:00am and 5:30pm

If there is any product demand during the holiday period, please try to release the order by January 10th, to ensure the punctual production and catch the final closing date. For any RFQs, NPD, and other issues, please send them to the corresponding contact window by Feb. 16, so that we can make response timely.

We're deeply sorry for any inconvenience that may cause you during this period. In case you have any urgent needs, please line me or give a call at 886-958-223355 at any time. Wish you a Happy New Year!

Thanks & best regards,
Wesley Yang

中文翻譯

親愛的顧客您好，

茲以本文通知您，倍斯特集團將為慶祝中國農曆年休假。請參閱全球據點之休假期間如下：

集團總部 -倍斯特國際貿易公司／臺灣臺北
休假期間：二月十八日星期三 至 二月二十二日星期日
恢復營運：二月二十三日星期一
辦公室 - 倍斯特公司／中國上海
休假期間：二月十八日星期三 至 三月五日星期四
恢復營運：三月六日星期五
發貨中心 - 倍斯特公司／美國密西根州的底特律
正常營運：時間 上午9：00 至 下午5：30

如果有任何在假日期間的產品需求，請儘量在一月十日前下單，以確保準時生產並趕上最後結關日。任何詢價、新產品開發，以及其它議題，請於二月十六日前提供予相應聯繫窗口，以便我司能及時作出反饋。

我司對在這一期間任何可能導致您的不便深感抱歉。如果您在這段時間有任何緊急需要，請隨時傳送即時通或撥打886-958-223355予我。祝您新年愉快！

衛斯理　楊　敬啟

知識補給

中國國慶七天休假稱「十一黃金週」（National Day Golden Week）或「國慶長假」，從十月一日起放；春節則稱為「春節黃金週」（Spring Festival Golden Week 或 Chinese Lunar New Year Golden Week）或「春節長假」。

職場經驗談

通常在中國農曆春節、大陸十一國慶及歐美聖誕假期前，買賣雙方皆會預先做好訂單規劃，即進口商做好訂單預估，而製造商則依據生產時程（production lead-time）估算需提前下單的時間點，避免因訂單集中湧入造成產能緊張，無法如期出貨之窘境。

菜鳥變達人

中翻英練習

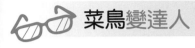

1. 我們因未達到您的目標價陷入膠著。

2. 記得回我電話。

中翻英解答

1 We are hard pressed to meet your target price.

2 Please be reminded to return my call.

3-1-3 人事異動
Reshuffle Announcement

★情境說明

Best Corp. notifies ABC Co. of the reshuffle of company staff.

倍斯特公司通知ABC公司有關公司人員異動訊息。

★角色介紹

（買方）Buyer: ABC Co., Ltd.
（賣方）Seller: Best International Trade Corp.

情境對話

B: Hello, I'm calling for Miss Olivia Porter.

B: 你好，我找奧利維亞・波特小姐。

A: Speaking. How can I help you?

A: 我就是。需要什麼協助嗎？

B: Please allow me to introduce myself. This is Wesley Yang from Best. I'm calling to notify you of Mr. Tony Yang's promotion, and it will be my great pleasure to take over his position to service you.

B: 請容我自我介紹。我是倍斯特的衛斯理 楊。我打電話來是通知您湯尼楊先生晉升的消息，而我將很榮幸接替他的職務服務貴司。

A: Hi, Wesley. Very pleased to meet you. I have heard a lot about you before.

A: 您好，衛斯理。很高興認識您，久仰大名了。

B: Same here. Here's the thing. I plan to personally visit you to discuss cooperation details next month.

B: 彼此彼此。是這樣的，我打算下個月親自拜訪您洽談合作細節。

A: Great. I look forward to meeting you in person.

A: 太好了！期待見到您本人。

B: So do I. Moreover, I were just sending you our updated quotation and catalogue of the new series, which you might be interested in.

B: 我也是。對了，我剛寄給您我們新系列產品最新的報價和目錄，你可能會感興趣。

A: Thank you. I'll take a good look at it.

A: 謝謝您！我會仔細看看。

B: Any time. Keep in touch!

B: 不客氣。保持聯繫！

關鍵字彙

promotion *(n.)* [prə`moʃən] 晉升

同義詞 advancement, exalt

相關詞 give a promotion 拔擢；demotion 降級

take over *(ph.)* 接管

同義詞 take charge of, takeover

相關詞 take over a company 接管公司；take over business 接管業務

position *(n.)* [pə`zɪʃən] 職位

同義詞 post, job, office

相關詞 eliminating positions 裁員（職位）；vacant position 空缺

same here *(ph.)* 彼此彼此；我也一樣

同義詞 same to you, so do I, me too

相反詞 I think not; I don't think so; I guess not 不以為然；我不認為如此

personally *(adv.)* [`pɝsn!ɪ] 親自

同義詞 in person, oneself, directly

相關詞 personally say 親口；take sth. personally 對某事不滿

be interested in *(ph.)* 對…感興趣；有意

同義詞 have interest in

相關詞 be interested in working abroad 有意從事外派的職務

相反詞 be indifferent to sth. 不聞不問（指不感興趣）

關鍵句型

take a good look at 仔細看一下

例句說明

Let's **take a good look at** earnings report of this month.

➡ 讓我們仔細看一下本月的財報。

You'd better **take a good look at** the quotation sheet before offering.

➡ 在報價前，你最好仔細看清楚。

替換句型

You'd better look the quotation sheet carefully before offering.

I have heard a lot about you. 久仰大名

例句說明

I have heard a lot about you. Pleased to meet you.

➡ 久仰大名，請多指教!

替換句型

I have heard so much about you. Nice to meet you.

I have heard a great deal about you. Glad to see you.

勵志小格言

Our greatest weakness lies in giving up. The most certain way to succeed is always to try just one more time.

~Thomas Edison, Inventor

我們最大的弱點就在於放棄。確保成功的最好辦法就是再試一次。

～發明家　湯瑪斯　愛迪生

英文書信這樣寫

Dear Customers,

This is to inform you that Mr. Tony Yang has been promoted to general manager of the Sales Department. We'd like to assign Mr. Wesley Yang to take over his position and be responsible for the trade issues between us.

Mr. Wesley Yang has been with Best Group more than ten years. He works seriously and tidy with original understanding and idea. We firmly believe his excellent ability and personal qualities will make great contributions to our future cooperation and consolidation of well trade relationship between two parties.

We would like to express our warmest thanks for your continued support throughout the years. Shall you have further questions and demands, please feel free to contact Wesley via wesleyyang@best.com.

Yours sincerely,
Best Group

中文翻譯

親愛的顧客您好，

茲以本文通知您，湯尼 楊先生已晉升為銷售部總經理。我司將委任衛斯理 楊先生接替他的職務，負責我們的貿易議題。

衛斯理 楊先生已在倍斯特集團服務逾十年。他工作嚴謹有條理，且見解獨到。我司堅信，他出色的能力和個人特質將對我們未來的合作，與鞏固雙方良好貿易關係上，作出巨大貢獻。

我司由衷感謝貴司多年來的持續支持。有進一步問題及需求，請隨時透過電郵 wesleyyang@best.com 與衛斯理聯繫。

倍斯特集團　敬啟

知識補給

人事異動種類英文說法：

1. 升職（promote）：Jack was promoted to the position of manager.
2. 降職（downgrade）：Jack was downgraded to the position of assistant manager.
3. 調職（transfer）：Jack, the manager of the Business Department, was transferred to another position.
4. 辭職（resign）：Jack, the manager of the Business Department, has resigned due to some personal reasons.
5. 免職（fire）：Jack, the manager of the Business Department, has been fired due to his negligence.
6. 退休（retire）：Jack has retired from the position of manager.
7. 留職停薪（take a leave of absence）：Jack, the manager of the Business Department, took a leave of absence due to some personal reasons.
8. 育嬰留職停薪（parental leave without payment）：Timmy, the section leader of the Business Department, was on parental leave without payment.

職場經驗談

就如同人員請假一樣，如逢人事異動時，人事單位或相關業務單位之主管應即時主動發函通知客戶，除說明異動原因外，主要是告知新的聯繫窗口（contact window），包含承接人員姓名、職稱、電話（分機）及電郵信箱等。尤其對國外客戶而言，無法直接至供應商端了解業務，因此透過電郵及電話聯繫特定業務人員是最直接的方式，所以客戶端通常不太樂見人員異動之情形，主要仍是擔心新承辦人員不熟悉及了解業務狀況。對於分工較細之企業，可提供聯繫窗口清單，包含各項業務負責人員，直屬主管及部門最高主管相關聯繫資料。

菜鳥變達人

中翻英練習

1. 驗貨員想仔細看一下巡檢紀錄。

2. 生管最好仔細看看出貨排程。

中翻英解答

1 The QC inspector would like to take a good look at the IPQC record.

2 The PCM would better to take a good look at the shipping schedule.

3-1-4 喬遷啟示
Removal Notification

★情境說明

Best Corp. notifies ABC Co. of the office relocation.
倍斯特公司通知ABC有關公司遷移訊息。

★角色介紹

（買方）Buyer: ABC Co., Ltd.
（賣方）Seller: Best International Trade Corp.

情境對話

B: This is Linda calling on behalf of Mr. Wesley Yang. May I speak with Miss Olivia Porter, please?

B: 我是琳達，代表衛斯理楊先生撥打此通電話。請問奧利維亞・波特小姐在嗎？

A: This is Olivia speaking. How may I help you?

A: 我是奧利維亞。有什麼需要我效勞的嗎？

B: I'd like to inform you of our headquarter relocation. The formal removal notification with the latest

B: 我想要通知您我司總部搬遷的事宜。正式的搬遷通知附上最新的公司

changes of our company will be emailed to you. Our email address remains unchanged.

變遷訊息會電郵給您。我司的電郵位址維持不變。

A: Got it. Thanks for your notification.

A: 知道了。謝謝您的通知。

B: Moreover, Mr. Yang told me to make sure that you will attend the commemoration party. He meant to invite you personally, but he must be housed up for a week with severe flu.

B: 另外，楊先生囑咐我要確定您會來參加慶祝派對。他本想親自邀請您，但他得到嚴重流感，需居家休養一周。

A: God bless him! Anything I can do for him, please be sure to let me know. Give him my best regards and let him know I will come.

A: 上帝保佑他！有什麼我能為他做的，請務必讓我知道。請代我問候他，並告訴他我會參加派對。

B: I will. Thanks for your concern.

B: 我會的。謝謝您的關心。

關鍵字彙

relocation *(n.)* [rilo`keʃən] **換位置；換地方**

同義詞 removal, changing location, moving to a new place

相關詞 relocation cost 搬遷費用；relocation plan 搬遷計畫

removal *(n.)* [rɪ`muv!] **搬遷；移動**

同義詞 relocation

相關詞 removal company 搬家公司；removal business 搬家業務

remain unchanged *(ph.)* **維持不變**

同義詞 stay the same, remain the same, be without change

相反詞 change back 恢復原樣；chop and change 不斷改變

attend *(v.)* [ə`tɛnd] **出席**

同義詞 be present, go to; show up

相關詞 attend a meeting 與會；attendance 出席人數；attendant 出席者

commemoration *(n.)* [kə͵mɛmə`reʃən] **紀念；慶典**

同義詞 remembrance, memorial

相關詞 commemoration day 紀念日；anniversary commemoration 周年紀念

meant to *(ph.)* **原本打算**

同義詞 intended to, was planning to, had intention of

相反詞 did not mean to, had no intention of；was not going to 原不打算

關鍵句型

be on behalf of sb. 代表某人

例句說明

I'm writing **on behalf of my supervisor** to express his appreciation.

➡ 我代表上司寫此文表達對您的感激之情。

Joe spoke **on behalf of her colleagues** to demand higher pay.

➡ 喬代表同僚發言要求加薪。

替換句型

Joe spoke in the name of her colleagues to demand higher pay.

A tell B to make sure… A要求B確定某事

例句說明

The manager told her assistance to make sure you'll present the meeting.

➡ 經理要求助理在下班前確定您會與會。

The buyer told the supplier to make sure the punctual shipment.

➡ 買方要求供應商確保準時出貨。

替換句型

The supplier was asked to insure the punctual shipment by the buyer.

勵志小格言

Good things come to those who believe; better things come to those who are patient; the best things come to those who don't give up.

~from website www.livelifehappy.com

好東西是帶給那些相信的人；更好的東西是帶給那些有耐心的人；最好的東西是帶給那些不放棄的人。

~摘錄至網頁 www.livelifehappy.com

英文書信這樣寫

Dear Customers,

We're glad to announce that Best Headquarter will move to a newly-built Formosa building with address and contact information as below. The new office will be in operation from May 01, 2015.

Headquarter - Best International Trade Corp. in Taipei Taiwan

Address: 20F.-G, No.100, Fuzhou St., Zhongzheng Dist., Taipei City, 10078 Taiwan, R.O.C.

Tel: 886-2-2351-6666

Fax: 886-4-2351-8888

Email: best.headquarter@best.com.tw

To express our immense gratitude of your continued support and cooperation for these years, we plan to hold afternoon-tea buffet at new office building from 2:00 PM to 5:00 PM on May 15.

The whole staff of Best sincerely look forward to your presence.

Yours sincerely,
Best Group

中文翻譯

親愛的客戶您好：

很高興的宣佈倍斯特總部即將遷移到新落成的福爾摩沙大廈，位址及聯絡資訊如下所列。新辦事處將於2015年5月1日啟用。

集團總部 -倍斯特國際貿易公司 / 臺灣臺北
10078臺灣臺北市中正區福州街100號20樓之G
電話：886-2-2351-6666
傳真：886-4-2351-8888
電郵：best.headquarter@best.com.tw

為表達我司對您這些年持續支持與合作的無限感激，我司計畫在五月十五日下午二點至五點於新辦公樓舉行自助下午茶會。

倍斯特全體同仁真誠期待您的蒞臨。

倍斯特集團　敬啟

知識補給

英文住址的寫法與中文相反，英文住址順序是由小至大，先寫門牌號碼、街名或路名，而後才是城市、州、郵遞區號，最後則是國家名。英文住址由小到大之順序如下：

樓 Floor（F或FL.）→ 號 Number（No.）→ 弄 Alley → 巷 Lane → 街 Street（St.）→ 路Road（Rd.）→ 段 Section（Sec）→ 區 District → 村 Village → 鄉 SHIANG → 鎮 JEN → 縣 SHIAN → 市 CITY

範例說明：

台灣台中市三民路二段100巷5弄100 號之20樓之2室

20F.-2, No.100, Aly. 5, Ln. 100, Sec. 2, Sanmin Rd., Central Dist., Taichung City 40041, Taiwan (R.O.C.)

台灣住址英譯及郵遞區號相關資料，可進入台灣郵政中文地址英譯的網頁查詢http://www.post.gov.tw/post/internet/Postal/index.jsp?ID=207

職場經驗談

目前與國外客戶訊息往來多已電子郵件居多，但仍會有需要藉由郵遞提供文件、樣品等其它資訊的情形。由我方寄件至國外，直接標註英文住址即可。但若由國外寄件至我方，則建議我方提供對方中、英文並列之住址，客戶可同時將中英文住址標註在收件人欄位，不僅可避免我方郵局或快遞公司因英譯差異導致誤送，亦可減少遞送之時間。

菜鳥變達人

中翻英練習

1. 凱特將代表倍斯特集團參加表揚大會。

2. 管理階層要求她確保做好準備並準時與會。

中翻英解答

1 Kate will attend the award ceremony on behalf of Best Group.

2 The management told her to make sure of getting everything ready and be present on time.

3-1-5 問卷調查
Questionnaire Survey

★情境說明

Best Corp. requests ABC Co to fill out the annual satisfaction questionnaire.

倍斯特公司需求ABC公司填寫年度滿意度調查表。

★角色介紹

（買方）Buyer: ABC Co., Ltd.

（賣方）Seller: Best International Trade Corp.

情境對話

A: Hi, Wesley. This is Olivia Porter at ABC Cooperation. You tried to reach me this morning?

A: 你好！衛斯理。我是ABC公司的奧利維亞 波特。您今早找我嗎？

B: Yeah. Your secretary said you was stepped out.

B: 是的。您的秘書說您外出。

A: I were out for lunch with customers. So, what's up?

A: 是呀！我外出與客戶用餐。那麼，有什麼事嗎？

B: Well. I want to thank you for all of your assistance and support to smooth our business during this year.

B: 是這樣的，我想感謝您提供的所有幫助與支持，使我們今年的業務能順利進行。

A: No, thank you for doing us a great favor, especially in disposing of our urgent demand. Your team did a good job!

A: 不，我才要感謝您幫了我們大忙，尤其是在處理我們的緊急需求上。您的團隊做得很好！

B: Oh, not at all. It's my duty. So if you have any suggestion or comment on our team or service, please don't hesitate to let me know by remarking in the annual satisfaction questionnaire.

B: 噢，您太客氣了。這是我的職責。所以如果您對我們的團隊或服務有任何建議或意見，請不要客氣備註在年度滿意度調查表中讓我知道

A: I'll be sure to let you know.

A: 我一定會的。

B: At any rate, appreciate for all you did.

B: 無論如何，感謝您所做的一切。

關鍵字彙

step out *(ph.)* 暫時外出

同義詞 go out, exit, leave

相關詞 step aside 讓開；out of step 不協調；step by step 循序漸進

smooth *(v.)* [smuð] 使順利

同義詞 lubricate, make even, make smooth

相關詞 smooth down 使平靜；smooth over 消除

dispose of *(ph.)* 處理

同義詞 manage, deal with, handle

相關詞 to dispose of a problem 解決問題；dispose of the spare time 打發空閒時間

duty *(n.)* [`djutɪ] 責任；本分

同義詞 responsibility, post, job

相關詞 off duty 下班；to be on duty 上班；be on duty 職勤

remark *(v.)* [rɪ`mɑrk] 評論；標註

同義詞 comment, mention, note

相關詞 remark measures 補救措施；remarks column 備註欄

at any rate *(ph.)* 無論如何

同義詞 in any case, in any event, at all events

相關詞 whatever it takes；at any cost 不計代價

關鍵句型

try to reach sb. 嘗試與某人取得聯繫

例句說明

Did **you try to reach the forwarder** to understand the status of rail strike?

➡ 你有試著聯繫貨代了解鐵路罷工的情形嗎?

The Purchasing Department has **tried to reach the material supplier** to urge the delivery.

➡ 採購部門已試著與原料供應商聯繫催促交期。

替換句型

The Purchasing Department has tried to get in touch with the material supplier to urge the delivery.

A wants to thank B for … A想向B表達…的謝意

例句說明

Our company wants to take this occasion to **thank you for** your assistance.

➡ 我司想藉此機會感謝您的協助。

Our company wants to thank all customers for their support.

➡ 我司要感謝所有客戶的支持。

替換句型

Our company want to appreciate all customers for their support.

勵志小格言

If I fail, I try again, and again, and again. If you fail, are you going to try again? The human spirit can handle much worse than we realize. It matters how you are going to finish.

~Nick Vujicic, Writer

如果我失敗了，我再試一次，再一次，再一次。如果你失敗了，你要再試一次嗎？人的精神可以處理比我們意識到的更糟。重要的是你要如何完成。

～作家　尼克　胡哲

英文書信這樣寫

Dear Customers,

Good day!

In order to offer you with the best service and quality meeting your needs, please fill in the attached Customer Satisfaction Questionnaire with any of your precious comments or suggestions, and email the scanned copy by return. We must process your valuable opinions seriously and carefully, and report to the top management.

In addition, please kindly let us know your sales programs of next year, so that we can prepare in advance to supply your need any time.

We hereby express our hearty gratitude for your respect and support.

Thank you and best regards,
Best Group

中文翻譯

親愛的顧客您好，

日安！

為了提供您最好的服務和品質，以滿足您的需求，請將您的任何寶貴意見或建議填入附件的客戶滿意度調查表中，並回傳掃描檔。我們必審慎及仔細的處理您寶貴的意見，並向最高管理階層稟報。

此外，請讓我們知道您來年的銷售計畫，如此我們可提前準備，因應您任何時間的所需。

謹此衷心感謝你的愛戴與支持。

感謝及誠摯的問候

倍斯特集團　敬啟

知識補給

年度客戶滿意度調查表範本:

Best International Trade Corp.
10F.-2, No.1, Fuzhou St., Zhongzheng Dist., Taipei City, Taiwan 10078
Tel: 886-2-2351-1111 / Fax: 886-4-2351-2222 /
Email: best.headquarter@best.com.tw

In order to help us offering better service for you, please take a few minutes to answer the following questions. Thank you!

∗What's your overall impression toward our products quality?
□excellent □very good □fair □poor □very poor Others__________

∗What is your overall impression toward our delivery schedule?
□excellent □very good □fair □poor □very poor Others__________

∗What's your overall impression toward our production lead-time?
□excellent □very good □fair □poor □very poor Others__________

∗What's your overall impression toward our product price?
□excellent □very good □fair □poor □very poor Others__________

∗What's your overall impression toward our communication?
□excellent □very good □fair □poor □very poor Others__________

∗Other comments and recommendations

____

____

Thanks for your time to complete the questionnaire. Please return us the scan copy, duly countersign. Best Group sincerely appreciate your respect and support.

職場經驗談

年度客戶滿意度調查表發送給客戶的時間點可在客戶年度假期之前兩至三週，如聖誕年假或新年年假，以利客戶有足夠時間回顧及彙整。

菜鳥變達人

中翻英練習

1. 我們要感謝您的耐心與理解。

---

2. 工廠試著聯繫銷售及生產部門協調生產及出貨事宜。

中翻英解答

1 We want to thank you for your patience and understanding.

2 The plant tried to reach Sales Department and Production Department to coordinate production and dispatch.

3-2 人際互動
Interpersonal Communications

3-2-1 表達祝賀
Expressing congratulations

★情境說明

Best Corp. expresses congratulations to the business partner in ABC Co. for his promotion.

倍斯特公司向ABC公司的合作夥伴表達對其晉升的祝賀之情。

★角色介紹

（買方）Buyer: ABC Co., Ltd.

（賣方）Seller: Best International Trade Corp.

情境對話

A: Hi, Tony. I'm calling to congratulate you on your promotion to the general manager.

A: 您好，湯尼。我打電話來祝賀您榮升為總經理。

B: The announcement have still not been officially issued. How do you get this message?

B: 公告尚未正式發佈。你怎麼得到這個消息的？

A: Good news travels fast.

B: I did not expect to be on the promotion list this year.

A: I wouldn't be surprised with the outstanding performance of your department.

B: It's the consummation of team work of Sales Department.

A: The success ascribes to your talent and leadership. I'm really pleasure to be working with an excellent partner like you.

B: It's also my pleasure. Really appreciate your call and congratulation to me.

A: 好事傳千里。

B: 我沒想到會在今年的晉升名單之列。

A: 對於貴部門的傑出表現，我並不感到意外。

B: 這是銷售部團隊合作的結果。

A: 這歸功於您的才能與領導。我真的很榮幸能與您這樣一位優秀的合作夥伴共識。

B: 也是我的榮幸。真的很感謝您致電祝賀我。

關鍵字彙

announcement *(n.)* [ə`naʊnsmənt] 布告

同義詞 proclamation, notice, notification

相關詞 official announcement 正式公告；place an announcement 刊登公告

issue *(v.)* [`ɪʃjʊ] 發布

同義詞 distribute, release, publish

相關詞 issue a newspaper 發行報紙；issue an order 法部命令

promotion list *(ph.)* 晉升名單

同義詞 advancement list；nomination list

相關詞 try for promotion 爭取晉升；be passed over for promotion 排除在升遷名單外

outstanding *(a.)* [`aʊt`stændɪŋ] 傑出的

同義詞 excellent, remarkable, significant

相關詞 be outstanding at 擅長於；an outstanding example 突出的例子

consummation *(n.)* [ˌkɑnsə`meʃən] 完成；成就

同義詞 accomplishment, performance, achievement

相關詞 consummation of the mission 完成任務；consummation of inventory system 完善的庫存系統

ascribe to *(ph.)* [əsˈkraib tu] 歸因於

同義詞 assign to, attribute to; impute to

相關詞 ascribe to oneself 賦予自己；ascribed role 賦予角色

關鍵句型

Sb. does not expect… 某人不預期…

例句說明

The manufacturer does not expect the price increasing of raw material.

➡ 製造商並無預期原物料價格上漲。

I don't expect to get the business.

➡ 我並不認為能談成這筆生意。

替換句型

I'm not supposed to get the business.

Sb. wouldn't be surprised… 某人對…不會感到意外

例句說明

I wouldn't be surprised to get the business.

➡ 我對於談成這筆生意並不會感到意外。

The manufacturer wouldn't be surprised for the price increasing of raw material.

➡ 製造商對於原物料價格上漲並不會感到意外。

替換句型

The price increasing of raw material wouldn't take manufacturer by surprise.

英文書信這樣寫

Dear Tony,

On behalf of ABC Co., I'd like to congratulate you on your promotion to the position of the general manager in the Sales Department.

Throughout recent years, you have expended a lot of effort to your company. It's your great talent leading to amazing performance of the Sales Department. All your hard work has not gone unnoticed. It's for sure that the department will become more prosperous under your management.

I wish you every success, and hope our cooperation will create magnificently in the future.

Yours sincerely,
Tom Smith

中文翻譯

湯尼您好：

僅代表ABC 公司祝賀您榮升為銷售部總經理。

這幾年您為公司投入了大量的心力。因為您的卓越才能，使銷售部門能有驚人的業績表現。您所有的努力沒有白費。可以肯定的是，在你的管理下，部門將更加繁榮。

祝您成功，並希望我們今後的合作會創造輝煌榮景。

湯姆　史密斯　敬啟

勵志小格言

They who know the truth are not equal to those who love it, and they who love it are not equal to those who delight in it.

~Confucious, Chinese thinker

知之者，不如好之者，好之者，不如樂之者。　*~中國思想家　孔子*

解析：對於學習事務的道理，僅是了解它的人，比不上喜愛他的人；喜愛他的人，又不如能樂在其中的人。

知識補給

向合作夥伴表示祝賀，可贈送禮品表達心意，禮品挑選時可投其所好，選擇收禮者喜愛的物品，當然這必須事先了解收禮者的喜好及習慣。再者若對對方不甚了解，則可依據當地習俗，挑選具有紀念意義、地方特色、宗教信仰或藝術價值之禮品。

但送禮仍有一定的講究及禁忌，例如國外客戶講究禮品包裝，而送禮要注意對等原則，贈送不同階級人員時，要注意位階及禮品規格要對等。另外各國對顏色、數字或花種的禁忌亦不相同，需事先了解，甚至宗教信仰的禁忌等都須納入考量，避免產生誤會。

而收禮者收到禮品時，需回函予客戶表達謝意。若為客戶當面贈送時，則應握手道謝。而歐美國家的習慣是收禮者可直接打開禮品表示讚美、喜愛及感謝之意。

職場經驗談

多數西方國家客戶對於具中國風的文物都相當感興趣，例如仿古古董文物、琉璃、玉飾等等。因此只要是東方色彩濃厚之禮品，都頗受西方客戶青睞。然而東風色彩文物多多少少會帶有宗教特色在，例如佛尊玉飾，因此宗教信仰仍是送禮時的必要考量之一，畢竟西方國家仍以信仰基督教居多。

菜鳥變達人

中翻英練習

1. 買方完全不期望以目標價格買到新品。

---

2. 執行長對於股價下跌並不感到意外。

中翻英解答

1 The buyer does not fully expect to buy this new product at the target price.

2 The CEO wouldn't be surprised to hear the news that shares fell.

3-2-2 表達弔唁
Expressing Condolence

★情境說明

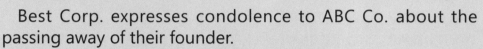

Best Corp. expresses condolence to ABC Co. about the passing away of their founder.

倍斯特公司向ABC公司表達對於其創辦人辭世的慰問之情。

★角色介紹

（買方）Buyer: ABC Co., Ltd.

（賣方）Seller: Best International Trade Corp.

情境對話

B: Hello, Olivia. This is Wesley over at Best. I were deeply sorry to learn that Mr. Kim Jackson passed away.

B: 你好，奧利維亞。我是倍斯特公司的衛斯理。我深感抱歉得知金姆傑克遜先生逝世。

A: Yeah. All of our staffs were also very shocked.

A: 是的。我們所有的員工也很震驚。

B: I have always admired Mr. Jackson's modesty and kindness. He was not only an admired entrepreneur, but also a generous scholar. I really

B: 我始終崇拜傑克遜先生的謙遜和仁慈。他不僅是一位令人欽佩的企業家，也是一個寬厚的學

learned a lot from Mr. Kim.

者。從金姆先生身上，我真的受益良多。

A: Thanks for your kind words.

A: 謝謝你的讚美。

B: All of us in Best who worked with him will never forget him. Please express our condolences to Jackson family.

B: 倍斯特公司所有與他共事過的員工將永遠不會忘記他。請向傑克遜家族表達我們的哀悼。

A: I will.

A: 我會的。

B: The God of love and peace shall be with you.

B: 慈愛和平的上帝必常與您們同在。

A: Thank you again for your call, Wesley. Your thought greatly supports us.

A: 謝謝您的來電，衛斯理。您的關懷給予我們極大的支持。

關鍵字彙

shock *(v.)* [ʃɑkt] **震驚；衝擊**

同義詞 frighten, terrify; shake

相關詞 demand shock 需求衝擊；shock-horror 駭人聽聞的

admire *(v.)* [əd`maɪr] **欽佩**

同義詞 honor, respect, revere

相關詞 admirer 愛慕者；to admire someone with the utmost sincerity 五體投地

modesty *(n.)* [`mɑdɪstɪ] **謙遜**

同義詞 humble, humility

相關詞 pleasing modesty 謙遜和善；characteristic modesty 謙遜特質

generous *(a.)* [`dʒɛnərəs] **慷慨的**

同義詞 unselfish, liberal, openhanded

相關詞 be generous with 在...方面很大方；generous offer 慷慨的資助

condolences *(n.)* [kən`doləns] **弔唁**

同義詞 expression of sympathy, commiseration, consolation

相關詞 condolence book 吊唁薄；memorial ceremony 追悼儀式

pass away *(ph.)* **逝世**

同義詞 pass on, expire, passing, die

相關詞 anniversary of the death 忌日；My condolences 節哀順變

關鍵句型

Sb. be deeply sorry for/that… 某人對…深感抱歉

例句說明

We were deeply sorry for the trouble we'd caused.

➡ 我們為所造成的麻煩深感抱歉。

The company was very sorry for any staff who was effected by the financial crisis.

➡ 公司對於因財務危機而受到影響的每位職工深感抱歉。

替換句型

The company felt very apologetic for any staff who was effected by the financial crisis.

express one's feeling to sb. 向某人表達情意

例句說明

I hardly know how to **express my anxieties to the plant** about the tight production capacity.

➡ 我真不知道如何向工廠表達我對於產能吃緊的擔憂之心。

The company should **express their regret to any staff** who was effected by the financial crisis.

➡ 公司應該向因財務危機而受到影響的每位職工表達歉意。

替換句型

Our company acknowledges you for bailing us out with economic aid to overcoming the financial crisis.

英文書信這樣寫

Dear Olivia,

I were deeply distressed to hear the passing way of your founder, Mr. Kim Jackson.

Mr. Jackson was not only an excellent leader, but also my admired elder. He made great contributions to the success of our cooperation during our company operating in the most difficult time. I were especially moved by his solicitude for subordinates and respect-treat to customers. No words can express my sympathies on losing such a nice person.

We all should follow his spirit and keep alive his example.

Yours sincerely,
Wesley Yang

中文翻譯

奧莉維亞您好：

聽聞貴司創始人金姆傑克遜先生與世長辭的消息，我深感不安。

傑克遜先生不僅是一位優秀的領導者，而且是我尊敬的長者。在我司經營最困難的時期，他為雙方成功合作做出巨大貢獻。令我特別感動的是他體恤下屬，尊重客戶。沒有任何言語可以表達我對失去如此善良者的傷痛。

我們都應遵循他的精神並以他為楷模。

衛斯理　楊　敬啟

勵志小格言

If you're walking down the right path and you're willing to keep walking, eventually you'll make progress.

~Barack Obama, the U.S. President

如果你走的道路正確，且願意堅持走下去，最終你就會進步。　*～美國總統　歐巴馬*

知識補給

西方國家信仰以基督教居多，因此喪禮遵循基督教儀式，主要色調為黑色，出席者衣著亦以深色服飾及配飾為主。喪禮由牧師或神父主持，大多在星期日舉行，方便親友參加，出席對象包含往生者之家屬、親友，或親友之朋友。而入殮儀式參加對象則以往生者家屬為主，主要是瞻仰往生者，見最後一面。

喪禮結束後即是出殯儀式，西方出殯儀式與東方佛教出殯儀式大致雷同，有樂隊、花車、家屬及親友跟隨靈車，出殯隊伍行進一段路程後，家屬會先行送別親友，而後由親屬進行最後安葬儀式。或也有親友一路隨行至近距離之墓園。

職場經驗談

無論是西方喪禮或東方喪禮，皆屬莊嚴隆重的場合，禮數上採致送輓聯、花圈、花籃或十字花架等，西方習俗上是在卡片上具名贈送者並題字「With Deepest Sympathy」，而卡片信封上是書寫往生者之姓名，如「To the Funeral of the Late Mr. Kim Jackson」。就商業關係來說，不太有機會出席國外客戶的喪葬禮，除了距離因素外，主要仍是親疏關係的考量，一般是發函表達對往生者的懷念及弔唁，當然如果商業合作夥伴同是至交好友，則另當別論。

菜鳥變達人

中翻英練習

1. 我們真的很抱歉擱置您的詢價如此長時間。

2. 請向貴司經理表達我對於貴司提供合作機會的感激之情。

中翻英解答

1 We are really sorry to keep your inquiry pending for so long.

2 Please express my gratitude to your manager offering the cooperation opportunity.

3-2-3 表達感謝
Expressing Appreciation

★情境說明

Best Corp. expresses appreciation to the customer for their hospitality during visitation to customer's company.

倍斯特公司感謝客戶於其參訪期間的招待。

★角色介紹

（買方）Potential Customer: NewTech Inc.
（賣方）Seller: Best International Trade Corp.

情境對話

B: Hi. I'm calling for Mr. Roger Douglas.	B: 您好！我找羅傑 道格拉斯 先生。
N: This is Roger speaking.	N: 我是羅傑 道格拉斯。
B: Hi, Roger. This is Wesley Yang from Best Co. I'm calling to thank you for your cordial hospitality during my visitation to your company.	B: 您好！羅傑，我是倍斯特公司的衛斯理・楊。我致電給您是要感謝您在我參訪貴司期間的熱情招待。
N: Quite welcome. The pleasure is ours.	N: 不客氣。是我的榮幸。

B: Deeply appreciate that we came to a mutual agreement in a short time. Welcome you as our customer to establish the relation of cooperation.

B: 非常感激我們雙方在如此短的時間內達到共識。歡迎你成為我們的客戶並建立合作關係。

N: The development of business is creditable to the cooperative plan you proposed to provide favorable conditions.

N: 此項生意的發展歸功於貴司的合作提案提供優惠條件。

B: That's is what we express to establish business relations with your firm.

B: 這表達了我們期盼與貴公司建立業務關係的渴望。

N: Quite sure.

N: 我相信如此。

B: BTW, I also enjoy the guided tour around your city. This place is nice and warm. Please must come to visit us and give me a chance to return the favor.

B: 對了，我同時享受於遊覽您所在城市。是個親切及溫暖的地方。請務必參訪我司，讓我有機會回報你的招待。

N: Certainly. I anticipate to visit you in soon.

N: 一定。我很期待近期內參訪貴司。

關鍵字彙

cordial hospitality *(ph.)* 殷勤招待

同義詞 cordial reception

相關詞 corporate hospitality 公司款待

mutual agreement *(ph.)* 共識

同義詞 reciprocal understanding

相關詞 mutual understanding 相互瞭解；mutual cooperation 互相合作

favorable condition *(ph.)* 優惠條件

同義詞 advantageous circumstance, auspicious condition

相關詞 favorable case 有利情形；favorable opportunity 好機會

關鍵句型

be creditable to 歸功於

例句說明

The development of business **is creditable to** your assistance.

➡ 業務的發展歸功於你的協助。

替換句型

All achievements are due to her support.

勵志小格言

Neither believe nor reject anything, because any other person has rejected of believed it. Heaven has given you a mind for judging truth and error, use it.

~By Thomas Jefferson, American president

不要因為別的人相信或否定了什麼東西，你也就去相信它或否定它。上帝贈予你一個用來判斷真理和謬誤的頭腦。那你就去運用它吧！ *～美國前總統　傑弗遜*

英文書信這樣寫

Dear Mr. Douglas,

I would like to take the advantage of this opportunity to bring my appreciation for your hospitality during my trip to your company.

I am really grateful for your help of making hotel reservation for me and showing me around your city. Your kindness made my trip very enjoyable, and your company team spirit also gave me deep impression. I sincerely hope that we can establish cooperation with each other in the near future.

No words can express my appreciation for you. I look forward to seeing you again soon.

Yours sincerely,
Wesley Yang

中文翻譯

道格拉斯先生您好：

藉由此信寫感謝您在我參訪貴司期間的熱情招待。

非常感謝您幫忙預定飯店及帶我參觀貴司所在城市。您的和藹可親使我的行程非常愉悅，貴司的團隊精神更令我印象深刻。我真誠地希望在不久的將來，我們雙方能建立合作關係。

任何言語都無法表達我對您的感激之意，期待很快再見到您。

衛斯理　楊　敬啟

知識補給

出訪客戶後向對方致上謝意為商業基本禮儀，發感謝函予對方，將使對方倍感窩心，內容勿冗長，簡要說明感激之情、說明具體原因及如何受惠，最後邀請對方參訪自家公司，並致上真誠祝福。切忌不宜在感謝函中提及其它實質業務，將使對方懷疑發文者的誠意。

職場經驗談

作為業務新手的您在初次拜訪客戶時難免不知所措，互相交換名片為第一步，名片交換要從位階最高的開始。接下來免不了寒暄話家常作為開場白，身為業務一定要隨身攜帶筆記及筆，即使是話家常，也可記錄對方談話，尤其針對第一次碰面的客戶這點更加重要，例如可記錄對方的生日、喜好、家人等等，待有機會時致上祝福或送份小禮物，將使對方備感溫馨，也可算是為日後商務合作關係奠定良好基礎。

菜鳥變達人

中翻英練習

1. 這筆訂單的促成，歸功於你的積極聯繫。

---

2. 請在任何您方便的時間回我電話。

中翻英解答

1 The achievement of this business is creditable to your aggressive connection.

2 please return my call at any time when it is convenient to you.

3-2-4 表達歉意
Expressing Apology

★情境說明

Best Corp. expresses apology to ABC Co. about the shipment postponement.

倍斯特公司向ABC公司表達對於出貨延遲的歉意。

★角色介紹

（買方）Buyer: ABC Co., Ltd.
（賣方）Seller: Best International Trade Corp.

情境對話

B: Hello, Olivia. This is Wesley Yang from Best.

B: 你好，奧利維亞。我是倍斯特的衛斯理 楊。

A: Hello, Wesley. I were on the point of calling you to ask about the shipment postponement.

A: 你好，衛斯理。我正要打電話給您詢問發貨延遲的事。

B: That's exactly why I am calling. Our QC found the critical dimensions of one production batch out of tolerance during IPQC. The dimension error was

B: 這正是我打電話來的原因。我司品管在巡驗時發現一批投產的關鍵尺寸超出公差。尺寸誤差

caused by the wrong path setting for processing cutting tool.

是由錯誤的加工刀具路徑設定造成的。

A: How's the defect rate?

A: 不良率為何？

B: One batch with 100% defect. Other two production runs passed AQL standard. I hate to tell you about this, but the urgent production still can't fulfill the shortage to catch up the punctual shipment. Really sorry.

B: 有一批百分百不良。其他兩批通過AQL檢驗標準。我很不想告訴您，但緊急投產仍不能補足短缺的數量趕上準時裝運。真的很抱歉！

A: That's too terrible. It's unacceptable for the shipment delay, as our customer needs the goods urgently.

A: 那太糟糕了。延遲交貨是不被接受的，我們的顧客急需這批貨。

B: How about arranging partial shipment for the verified batches as scheduled? The rest goods will be sent by air freight at our cost.

B: 不如安排分批如期出貨合格品。剩下的產品由我司付費空運出貨。

A: Well, I suppose there's no alternative.

A: 看來我別無選擇。

B: I'm terribly sorry. I really am.

B: 我很抱歉！真的很抱歉！

關鍵字彙

critical *(a.)* [ˋkrɪtɪk!] **關鍵的；重要的**

同義詞 important, crucial, capital

相關詞 self-critical 嚴以律己的；critical period 關鍵期

tolerance *(n.)* [ˋtɑlərəns] **公差；容限**

同義詞 endurance, common difference, allowance

相關詞 tolerance range 公差範圍；damage tolerance 損傷容限

IPQC *(ph.)* **（In process quality control）制程檢驗；巡檢**

相關詞 FAI (First Article Inspection) 首件檢驗；首檢

解析 制程檢驗是指為防止不合格品流入下一道工序，對各道工序加工的產品及主要工序進行檢驗。並根據檢測結果判定產品是否符合規格及判定工序是否處於穩定。

pass *(v.)* [pæs] **通過**

同義詞 approve, succeed, do well

相關詞 guard a pass 把關；pass an entrance test 考取；let it pass 算了

unacceptable *(a.)* [ˏʌnəkˋsɛptəb!] **無法接受的；令人不滿的**

同義詞 unsatisfactory, undesirable, discontented

相關詞 unacceptable behavior 不被接受的行為；totally unacceptable 完全無法接受；unacceptable risk 不可接受的風險

verified *(a.)* [ˋvɛrəˏfaɪd] **已證實的；已檢驗的**

同義詞 confirmed, proved to be true；substantiated

相關詞 verified copy 經驗證的副本；verified license 驗證許可證

關鍵句型

Sb. be on the point of　某人正想要

例句說明

The HR is on the point of calling the interviewee.

➡ 人事正要打電話給面試者。

The interviewer was on the point of leaving when the interviewee finally came.

➡ 當面試者終於趕來時面試官正要離開。

替換句型

The interviewer was about to leave when the interviewee finally came.

A hate to tell B about sth., but…　A不想告訴B某事卻不得不…

例句說明

The seller always hates to tell the buyer about price rises, but the rising costs have made it hard to go on with the business.

➡ 賣方總是不願告知買方漲價的事，但成本上升已造成生意經營困難。

The company hates to tell the staff about the layoff signal, but the financial crises have badly impacted the operation.

➡ 公司不願告知員工裁員的訊息，但財務危機已衝擊公司營運。

替換句型

The company cannot help but telling the staff about the layoff signal, as the financial crises have badly impacted the operation.

英文書信這樣寫

Dear Olivia,

Please accept our sincere apology for the delay in delivering your order. The power cuts without the prior notice caused the tight capacity last month. To make matters worse, our emergency generators conked out and were unable to run efficiently even after repair.

We have worked an extra shift to rush out your order last week and are sure to make the shipment tomorrow morning.

Once again, we awfully regret for the great inconvenience we have caused. Your kind understanding of our position will be appreciated.

Yours sincerely,
Wesley Yang

中文翻譯

奧利維亞您好，

對於延遲出貨貴司訂單，請接受我司誠摯的歉意。上個月無預警的停電是造成產能吃緊的原因。更糟的是，我們的應急發電機出現故障，即便在維修後也無法有效運轉。

我司已在上星期加班趕製貴司訂單，並保證明天早上發貨。

對於我司所造成的不便，再次致歉。您能理解我司的立場，將不勝感激。

衛斯理　楊　敬啟

勵志小格言

Life is not a semester system, life without summer vacation, and no employer to help you find self-interest, use their spare time to do it now!

~Bill Gates, Microsoft co-founder

人生不是學期制，人生沒有寒暑假，沒有哪個雇主對幫助你找到自我有興趣，請立即用自己的空暇做這件事吧！

～微軟創辦者　比爾蓋茲

知識補給

出貨延後是客戶最不想得知的訊息，其造成的原因大多數為生產管理因素所造成，此通常亦為客戶較不能接受之原因，因此出貨無法及時所導致之相關損失或費用，客戶端保有向供應端索賠之權利。但如因氣候等天然災害因素所致，如在亞洲地區夏季常出現之颱風，則屬不可抗力因素，除非另有其它原因，一般來說不可歸咎於出口商。

而遭逢臨時天然災害休假，應由業務單位或人事單位統一發出緊急休假通知予客戶，而因休假所致之相關業務影響，則由各單位負責人員各別細項通知客戶。簡要颱風假（typhoon day off）通知如下:

Dear Sirs,

This is to inform you that our office will be closed for typhoon day off on September 1. The office will resume on September 2.

In case there is any urgent matter, please send your message to our mail box. We shall be at your services as soon as possible.

Yours sincerely,
Best Group

職場經驗談

在大陸內地地區夏季因電力供應吃緊，經常會有無預警之停電，雖各企業為能有所應變多數會在自己廠區內加設發電機等電力供應設備，但仍或多或少會影響正常生產及出貨，因此訂單業務在與生產管理單位協調訂單排程時，需將相關風險納入考量，避免影響交期。

菜鳥變達人

中翻英練習

1. 我打給大衛時，他正要登機。

---

2. 我不願告知客戶包裝錯誤的事，但這批貨物已結關並離港。

中翻英解答

1 David was on the point of boarding the plane when I called.

2 I hate to tell the customer about the wrong package, but the shipment has already been cleared through customs.

3-2-5 表達慰問
Expressing Solicitude

★情境說明

Best Corp. expresses solicitude to ABC Co. suffering in the natural disaster.

倍斯特公司向ABC公司表達對其遭遇天然災害的慰問之情。

★角色介紹

（買方）Buyer: ABC Co., Ltd.
（賣方）Seller: Best International Trade Corp.

情境對話

A: Good afternoon. ABC Cooperation. This is Linda Ryder.

A: 下午好。這裡是ABC公司，我是琳達 萊德。

B: Hello. This is Wesley Yang at Best. I'd like to speak with Olivia.

B: 您好，我是倍斯特公司的衛斯理 楊。我找奧利維亞。

A: I'm sorry to let you know that Olivia was admitted to the hospital with leg fracture due to the tornado.

A: 很抱歉告知您奧利維亞遭受龍捲風襲擊因而腿部骨折住院。

B: Oh, my. I'm deeply sorry to hear this bad news. Is she alright?

B：噢，天啊！聽到這個壞消息，我深感抱歉。她還好嗎？

A: She still needs to be hospitalized for a week.

A: 她仍然需住院一週。

B: I just saw the TV news about the terrible tornado and thought to call her. I were unexpected to hear of her poor incident.

B: 我剛剛看到這可怕龍捲風的電視新聞，想到要致電給她。我很意外聽到她的噩耗。

A: The news also gave us a shock.

A: 這個消息也讓我們很震驚。

B: Please give my concern to her, if you see her.

B: 如果您見到她，請向她表達我的關心之情。

A: Thank you, Mr. Yang. I will. BTW, I'll take care of her work, while Olivia stay in hospital. Any requirement, please let me know.

A: 謝謝你，楊先生。我會的。對了，在奧利維亞住院期間，我會接手她的工作。有任何的需求，請讓我知道。

關鍵字彙

speak with *sb.(ph.)* **與某人談話討論**

同義詞 talk with, discuss with

相關詞 speak with a forked tongue 花言巧語；speak up 暢所欲言

admit *(v.)* [əd`mɪt] **准許進入；承認**

同義詞 allow entrance, receive；acknowledge, recognize

相關詞 admit defect 甘拜下風；cannot admit of doubt 不容置疑

alright *(a.)* [`ɔl`raɪt] **沒問題的；健康的**

同義詞 great, very well, fine

相關詞 getting on alright with sth. 某事發展順利；just alright 還好

hospitalize *(v.)* [`hɑspɪtl̩͵aɪz] **住院治療**

同義詞 hospitalize, place in a hospital, admit into a hospital

相關詞 hospitalized for observation or home quarantine 留院觀察或居家隔離

hear of *(ph.)* [hiəɔv] **聽到；知悉**

同義詞 hear about, listen to

相關詞 hear out 聽完；hear said 聽說過；hear tell of sth. 聽人說起某事物

take care of *(ph.)* **照顧；處理**

同義詞 look after, watch over, guard over

相關詞 take care of trade business 處理外貿業務

關鍵句型

Sb. thought to… 某人想到要…

例句說明

John didn't think to receive the sample.

➡ 約翰沒想到會收到樣品。

I thought to bring John a sample.

➡ 我想到要帶個樣品給約翰。

替換句型

It occurred to me to bring John a sample.

Sb. be unexpected to hear of 某人無預期聽到

例句說明

I am unexpected to hear of her resign.

➡ 我無預期會聽到她辭職的消息。

Although we perceive the financial crisis does badly impact the industry operation, **we are unexpected to hear of** your firm collapsed.

➡ 即便知道金融危機確實影響產業經營，但我們無預期聽到貴司倒閉的消息。

替換句型

Hearing about your firm collapsed is beyond our expectation, even if we knew the financial crisis did influence the industrial operation.

英文書信這樣寫

Dear Olivia,

I'm writing to make sure everything is OK after the tornado whirled into your city this week. All of us in Best feel deeply sorry to learn this terrible disaster and must tell you how much we sympathize with you, your family, and your country.

I sincerely hope that all can make a quick recovery. Should you need any assistance during this difficult period, please feel free to let me know. We must do our best to support you with any assistance.

One again, please express our sympathy to all of your family and colleagues. Best will be always with you.

Yours sincerely,
Wesley Yang

中文翻譯

奧利維亞您好，

我寫信是要確定在本週歷經龍捲風席捲您們城市後，您們一切安好。所有倍斯特同仁對於這個可怕的災難深感遺憾，必須告訴您，我們對於您、您的家人、及您的國家深表同情。

衷心地希望一切能很快復原。您在這個困難時期需要任何協助，請隨時讓我知道。我們必竭盡所能支援您任何協助。

請代為向您所有的家人和同事表達同情之意。倍斯特永遠與您同在。

衛斯理　楊　敬啟

勵志小格言

If you run into a wall, don't turn around and give up. Figure out how to climb it, go through it, or work around it.

~Michael Jordan, NBA player

如果你碰到一堵牆，不要轉身放棄。找出如何爬上去，穿過它，解決它的方法。

～*NBA* 球員　麥可・喬丹

知識補給

休假通常分為帶薪假(paid leave)及無薪假(unpaid leave)兩類，依據各企業經營時間，企業給予員工之帶薪假一般有週休(weekend off)、隔週休(bi-weekend off)、調修(adjusted holiday)、補修(compensatory holiday)及特休(annual leave)。如下所列之人事假給薪與否則依各企業規定。

事假 Personal Leave
病假 Sick Leave
公假 Official Leave
婚假 Marriage Leave
喪假 Funeral Leave
產假 Maternity Leave
產前假 Pre-Maternity Leave
陪產假 Paternity Leave
流產假 Miscarriage Leave
生理假 Menstruation Leave
家庭照顧假 Family Care Leave
公傷假 Occupational Sickness Leave
值日假 Deferred Leave for Guard Duty
加班假 Deferred Leave for Working Overtime

職場經驗談

一般人事休假，個人可在休假前設定電子郵件系統自動發出休假通知予客戶，或由個人或人事單位發送信函告通函予客戶，除了告知休假期間，另一個重點是在通知中說明人員休假期間之職務代理人相關聯繫資訊。

菜鳥變達人

中翻英練習

1. 採購部門剛想到要致電給供應商確認交期。

2. 採購部門無預期聽到交期延後的消息。

中翻英解答

1 The Purchasing Department just thought to call the material supplier about the delivery date.

2 The Purchasing Department was unexpected to hear of the shipment delay.

Leader 014

國貿 B.C.S.英語：A 咖國貿人

（深植就業力+升值職場競爭力）

作　　者　施美怡
封面構成　高鍾琪
內頁構成　菩薩蠻數位文化有限公司

發 行 人　周瑞德
企劃編輯　劉俞青
執行編輯　陳韋佑
校　　對　陳欣慧、饒美君
印　　製　大亞彩色印刷製版股份有限公司
初　　版　2015 年 3 月
定　　價　新台幣 369 元
出　　版　力得文化
電　　話　(02) 2351-2007
傳　　真　(02) 2351-0887
地　　址　100 台北市中正區福州街 1 號 10 樓之 2
E-mail　best.books.service@gmail.com

港澳地區總經銷　泛華發行代理有限公司
地　　址　香港新界將軍澳工業邨駿昌街 7 號 2 樓
電　　話　(852) 2798-2323
傳　　真　(852) 2796-5471

國家圖書館出版品預行編目(CIP)資料

國貿英語業務篇 / 施美怡作. -- 初版. -- 臺北市 : 力得文化, 2015.03
面 ; 公分. -- (Leader ; 14)
ISBN 978-986-91458-3-1(平裝)

1.商業英文 2.會話

805.188　　104002384